DEDICATION FROM JO

The Hunter's Arrow Ltd was a dream made possible through friendship. Without those friendships, the stories which we hope you will enjoy would never have come together. So, thanks go to the following:

> Tracy Andrews
> Donna DeBoard
> Bethan Thomas
> Gabriela Collazo
> Angela Keys
> Melissa Keyza
> Katlyn Bosch
> Aiden Williams

I am fortunate to have such creative and innovative friends. If we have learned anything it is that a dream can come true. We are much more than our detractors might say, and through our stories, we have proven just how wrong they are. I look forward to writing with you for many years to come.

I also want to thank those non-writers, who have told me how much they enjoy what I have written from the early days of writing online role-play and fan fiction, to now. Your encouragement and support means the world to me.

Finally, my thanks to Karen Nethercott, Marta Jenkala and Miss TN Kiersnowska: three teachers from St Anne's Convent School. In your own way, you started me down the journey of writing.

My friends, you all rock!

MEMORIES OF AN EIGHTEENTH BIRTHDAY GIFT

"There are two sides to every story, even mine"

It was the reason that the Ring had a sanded floor, to make the removal of post-punishment detritus easier. But this was different, Casimir knew, as he lifted the rope barrier to duck under, the strands grazing his bare shoulders as he did so. This was more, but then, it was only fitting considering the purpose. The Ring was for the punishment of those who had invoked the displeasure of their Alpha. The Ring was a place for those foolish enough to cross Pierre Gosselin to learn the error of their ways, and more often than not, it would be at the hands of the second son, Casimir.

Was he the Psycho Gosselin that had been his whispered nickname since his rumoured murder of his sibling, Charles. He had not even been sixteen, when he returned for winter training in the Laurentians, without his brother. An unfortunate victim of a failure to prepare for the harsh conditions. That had been the official explanation. Pierre Gosselin had mourned very publicly that he had lost a beloved son, but those within the Pack were not fooled. As his father had mourned, Casimir had stood, two paces behind his father's left shoulder, his face impassive. No emotion. No grief. No joy. Nothing. Sixteen years old, and, clearly, his soul was as dead as his late brother. So they said. Psycho. One whose leash was barely held by his sire, it was rumoured.

Now this. Not a Ring, but a field, the grass clipped neatly that one might almost think it was a lawn for picnics, parties and games. This was a game, if your ideas were twisted. This was a party, a celebration of birth, but the joyful outcome, for most of those inside the rope, was far from certain. Pain. Despair. A

3

loss of hope. A sense of inevitability. For some, a determination, to give as good as they received. But for most, their hope ended, a shrivelled memory, when the birthday boy entered the ring, barefoot, unarmed, shirtless, clothed in white, cotton, martial-arts style trousers. Pristine white, in contrast to his black soul.

A birthday party for the celebrated second son. "Happy Eighteenth Birthday to you", Casimir ignored the sardonic tone of the voice in his mind. Since Charles' death, this had been his norm. Several months ago, the sessions in the Ring had stopped, and a rumour confirmed that transgressors would meet their fate here, in this mockery of the Roman Coliseum. Weapons littered the grass, between the eighteen 'challengers' and Casimir, where he stood at the centre. The challengers wore shackles and manacles, the electronic locks set to release at the appropriate time. The theory was clear. Casimir stood alone. Unarmed. The weapons were there. Take the weapons. Be the one to strike down the Psycho Gosselin, and be the one to take his place as Beta-In-Waiting to his eldest brother, the First Son and Heir.

Putting the theory into practice? Well, that was a different matter.

CHAPTER 1 – WELCOME TO MY NEW HOME

I was known as the Psycho Gosselin. It was a name I had earned. It was a name which cost me dearly, but in gaining that name others benefited. I am sure that must sound strange. How would it be possible others to benefit from the fact that I was known as a stone-cold-hearted killer? Make no mistake that was the nature of my nickname. The Psycho Gosselin. I was the second born son of my sire at least in terms of his acknowledged offspring but where others considered my elder brother to be my sire's heir in terms of gaining the title of Alpha of the Gosselin Pack, I think it is safe to say that I was the one that they truly feared. As I grew into adult hood, those who knew my sire and his attitudes towards what constituted legitimate business, knew also that if my sire failed to have his way, he would not hesitate to deploy "his deterrent". His deterrent. That was what I was seen to be. But therein lies the question. Was that all I was, or was there more? Yes, you say, of course he would try to justify what he has done. That is the mind of a psychopath. All I ask is that you judge me only after you have read my side of the story. That is all I ask.

By the time I was fifteen, I had gained the nickname of Psycho Gosselin. Ten years had passed since I had arrived in my sire's home. Technically, it was the home of his mate, Janice Gosselin. My dam had told me it was my birth-right that I should be recognised as the get of Pierre Gosselin, which was why she took me to Pierre one morning, told my sire I was his responsibility, spun on her heel and left. When Pierre sent one of his assistants to find her, she had disappeared. No scent trail could be found. My looks made it clear that I was my sire's get, but it didn't mean that this was an easy process. Birth-right? That was a term that made no sense to a child, who until then, had lived with his dam. We had lived within the Pack, it was true, but we had been lower ranking members. My dam had been a Canadian Native, who had caught my sire's eye. No one in their right mind turned down the attentions of Pierre Gosselin and my dam was no fool. I was the result of what had been merely a dalliance for the Alpha Designate and new mate of the incumbent Alpha's daughter. Why would he risk his position when given time, the whole Pack would be his to command? Unlike Laurent's dam, my own dam did not draw attention to the identity of my sire, but as I grew, as my features developed, it was clear to any who chose to look at a mere pup.

It was hardly surprising that I held Laurent in low regard. His dam would bruit that he was the only offspring of Pierre Gosselin, that it was time for him to put aside Janice since she had not borne him any live young. She had proven that she could. The incumbent Alpha's health was faltering. He had accepted Pierre into his family after Pierre avowed that he would honour his mating with Janice Gosselin. As a show of his good intent, he changed his own name to Gosselin, that the name of the Pack would continue. Given the size of the Pack, it was important to have a strong Alpha at the helm and that was what the new Alpha Designate was offering. Stability and strength. For all intents and purposes, the mating between Pierre Gosselin and the former Alpha's only female offspring, Janice, was a love match. Perhaps it was in the early days, but that was before I was born and before I came to know the truth about that particular mating.

My life would change when Pierre Gosselin acceded to the title of Alpha. He had been mated to Janice for two years by then, but as was so often pointed out by Laurent's dam, she was yet to produce an heir to her blood-line. Her mate and our new Alpha had decreed that, in the interests of a strong succession for the pack's benefit, he would recognise his male pups as his heirs. So, Laurent was brought to the house, as was I, and our sibling, Charles, who was younger than me by one month.

Time to wake up. In under a day, I went from being a low-ranking pup whose dam had caught the Alpha's eye once, to the recognised second son and 'spare' heir to the Alpha. My elder brother, Laurent, was of course the heir to the Gosselin Pack, and his training as Alpha Designate would start immediately. Ultimately, he would take on the role of Beta, whilst I would be his loyal and capable assistant so that when he acceded to the rank of Alpha, I would be his loyal Beta. But first things first. We must both be quartered as befitted the sons of Pierre Gosselin and that meant in his mate's home, under her nose, a constant reminder of her barren state. That was how my sire described it when, in a rare show of spirit, she had expressed her reluctance to grant us the welcome our sire felt appropriate.

"You barren bitch!" My sire had struck Janice across the face, knocking her into the panelled wall of the hallway. "You can't provide me with heirs, so I am fortunate others don't have that pathetic disability." He had snarled at her as she crouched against the wall, shielding her bruised face and already blackening eye from further blows. "You will make MY sons welcome." He had smiled, and there was real anticipation in that smile. "Or, I will have to show you the price of disobedience."

Janice had nodded, pulling herself to her feet. She had looked at the three of us: Laurent stood with his legs braced, his arrogance apparent; I stood strong, as my dam had told me I must; Charles stood slightly behind me, but then, he lacked the arrogance of Laurent or my own ability to mimic confidence.

Welcome to my new home. Yeah, right.

CHAPTER 2 – JUST ANOTHER PUP

There was a time when I was just another pup. For the first six years of my life, I lived with my dam. When I moved in with my sire, it did not occur to me that I never questioned the belief that my dam had died. I knew she had died, otherwise, why would I be living with my sire? But for those first six years of my life, I did have a dam. I lived with my mother.

It was not uncommon for pups to be born to unmated females. We were shifters. We lived with the seasons and when a female was in heat, she was in heat. Simple as that. Even as a pup I knew that. My dam did not seem to be upset if a male wished to run with her. 'Run' was understood to be another way of saying 'mate' with her.

I was four years old when Pierre Gosselin took over the Alpha position of the Gosselin Pack, with the death of Janice's sire. Change did not come immediately. To start with, he had to convince the previous Alpha's advisors and supporters that he intended to fulfil the promises he had made to his predecessor. He had made many promises indeed. There were many who felt that as the previous Alpha had aged, the Gosselin Pack had lost some of its influence in shifter circles. Make no mistake the Gosselin Pack was a large pack, influential not just in terms of financial wealth but in terms of the geography covered by the pack territory. So even a perceived loss of influence was a major issue. Who was Pierre Gosselin? He had the looks, he had the strength of physique and he had undoubted charisma. He wooed Janice Gosselin, the only daughter of the Gosselin Alpha and he had promised her the moon and stars. Of course, I did not know this is a child, but when I was older, Janice admitted to me how easy it had been to be taken in in those early days. It had been so easy her to believe that this charismatic and handsome male wanted her for more than the fact that she was the only living offspring of the Gosselin Alpha. So yes, Pierre Gosselin made a lot of promises, some of them intended to maintain the status quo and some of them intended to bring changes which some of the pack felt were all too necessary.

The easiest to keep had been changing his name to Gosselin. This was the Gosselin Pack. It was a large pack, cash rich and land rich. The pack was influential with the Shifter Council. Pups were educated and trained in how to contribute to the wellbeing of their Pack. This was all very well established, but Pierre Gosselin had to demonstrate that he would keep his word. In a pack as numerous as the Gosselin Pack, it was not sufficient that he satisfied those who want to change. He had to take the rest of the adults with him, or, he had to find a solution to their dissent. He had to promise that he would listen to them, that he would understand their concerns and that he alone would be in a position to effect the changes that were necessary for the Gosselin Pack to both maintain its status and to continue to grow its status. That's what he told them. That is what they believed.

At least, he kept his word until the 'accidents' started to happen. As I have said, we are wolves. We are shifters and we are not weak creatures. But the accidents happened. A moonlit pack run and hunt, and a wolf might slip on a shale slope. The Laurentian Mountains in winter were not a forgiving place, and due care was always needed. My dam always used to keep me towards the rear of the pack during such runs, taking care that I was able to enjoy the run, rather than have to worry about the potential politics. Even at four years old, when in my human form, I had some similarities in looks to my sire, but I also had my dam's darker hair. Perhaps this meant that I was not noticed so much, not like my half-brother, Laurent.

His dam's approach was completely different. She made no bones about the fact that her pup was the eldest pup sired by the new Alpha. She had plans and they did not include Janice Gosselin producing a pup of her own bloodline, not when she had borne Pierre a strong and healthy pup in Laurent. So how did this affect Laurent as a pup? It was inevitable, really.

Laurent was a matter of months older than me, but his attitude was that he was the get of Pierre Gosselin, and once his sire became the Alpha in truth, he made it clear amongst his age-mates that in time, he would be the next Alpha.

This was bound to have an effect on the informal hierarchy amongst the pups of the Pack. The young of most species learn by copying the behaviour of adults. Laurent's, and thus by effect, my behaviour would be no different.

CHAPTER 3 - LAURENT

Humans would have seen something similar: the popular kid in a school, the captain of a sports team. There are always situations where there is jostling for ranking and an eye on what was to come. Pick on the weak, follow the strong. That is the nature of pack, surely? Or is it? Watch wild wolves and there is scope for challenge but there is also order. What was Laurent doing? In retrospect, I might give an opinion, but I am not writing this from an adult's perspective. I am writing this as I recall from my childhood memories.

As a pup, what did I see? I saw a bully. I saw a male pup who was physically bigger than others, because his dam would ensure that he ate well. She made sure that she maintained Pierre Gosselin's interest in her physically, and that meant that her sturdy male pup was constantly in his sire's regard. Her voice used to grate on my ears, I recall, making me wince, but it was a reaction that my dam would caution me to hide. A wince, even slightly, could be considered a sign of weakness. My dam may have kept us to the rear of pack runs, but that did not make her weak, and I recall at least one occasion when either one of the other females or a male whom she did not favour tried to force her to their will. Make no mistake, my dam could and did fight to maintain her standing. But returning to the subject of Laurent. No, I didn't like my sibling, not even then. I had a vague recollection of how the previous Alpha had been, and it seemed wrong. It seemed off somehow, but as a pup, I could not have said why it felt wrong, only that it did.

It was inevitable that Laurent would try to play his dominance 'games' with me. After all, I was a matter of months younger, and given how vocal his dam had been, everyone knew that he was Pierre Gosselin's get, even if it was not acknowledged in public. Or should I say, it was not acknowledged whilst the old Alpha still lived. Once he was dead, then the entire pack knew that things would change. Such is the nature of Pack.

Laurent and I were different body types, even in human form. We were both grey wolves when shifted, but he was stockier than I was, although I was taller. As was the norm, we took part in physical training. To a human, such training might have seemed excessive, given that I was only just shy of being five years old. Laurent was nearer to six years old, a point he was heard to emphasise repeatedly, along with, yes as you might have guessed, the fact that he was his sire's get. What caused the fight? I can't recall the circumstances. What mattered was the outcome, because I did not bow down to him, or show throat as was appropriate for a pup submissive to him.

We were sparring. Yes, even as pups we were involved in full contact sparring, because whilst we might have seemed to be children by human standards, we were anything but by shifter standards. More to the point, it could never be said that the get of Pierre Gosselin did not know how to fight. It was all about dominance, which of us was a worthy legacy of our sire. That was what mattered, hence us fighting full contact. Supposedly, the fight was under the supervision of the instructors and given that the old Alpha still lived, there was more control that became the norm when Pierre took over as Alpha. But I have skipped ahead.

This fight, a cross between wrestling and anything goes: punches, kicks, distraction techniques. With Laurent, it was more a case of 'anything goes'. His mind had been filled with his dam's constant harping that he was the eldest offspring of Pierre Gosselin and he wanted all the younglings to see him, in effect, as the Alpha pup. Such a shame that I had no intention of letting that happen. I had no wish, even then to be subservient to my brother. Little more than a bully, I might not match him physically, but I could out-manoeuvre him tactically instead and that was what I did.

Laurent favoured using his height and weight advantage but being of lighter build, I was faster of my feet, and I had learned to use my body to my advantage when faced with a larger opponent. It was a matter of using my hips, pushing them under Laurent to act as a pivot for a throw. When I flipped Laurent on his back, using his bulk against him, I had my hand around his throat, albeit only for a minute and it was not seen by the adult instructor. But Laurent knew that I had had him on his back and I had held him by the throat. It sat ill with him, and that was putting it mildly. I knew he would try again. I might have been adjudged by the instructor to have won that bout, but I knew that Laurent would not be satisfied. Siblings we might have been, but there could be only one dominant pup. He would try again.

CHAPTER 4 – DOMINANCE FIGHTS

He tried to attack me when I was waiting my turn for one-to-one tuition with one of the teachers, going through some of the basic drills that we were being taught. There were a lot of us, and I suspect that was why the fight was not stopped. Or maybe it was not stopped because the adults knew that Laurent was the eldest and that we were both sired by Pierre Gosselin. I don't know, and it didn't matter. One moment, I was concentrating on my drills and the next the grey wolf form of Laurent barrelled into me, knocking me across the training ring until I came to a stop by one of the pillars.

I sprang to my feet immediately, or rather to my paws. My shifts had always been fast, and with the hindsight of adulthood, the reason for that was clear because of my bloodline. And, I don't mean the blood of Pierre Gosselin. Snarling, I turned on my attacker, registering that it was Laurent, and also registering that he hadn't expected me to respond by coming to fight stance. He snapped at me, a clear 'back-down' instruction. Well, to hell with that! He attacked me, and my instincts were screaming for me to demonstrate that I wouldn't take that lying down. I had no intention of showing throat. My returning snarl was louder and I, too, snapped my jaws in an equally clear, "Try it!" response. We circled each other. Laurent lunged at me, snapping again. A feint, rather than an actual attack. I returned the gesture. I might not be attacking him, yet, but I was not giving in to him either.

I felt a mental brush which was my dam, more of a question. My response was non-verbal, a mental image of pup to dam that Laurent had attacked first. I felt her agreement. I couldn't back down. I must remember that I was as much my sire's get as Laurent. For my future in the pack, I had to make clear that I was no pushover. There was a flurry of movement to the side, and I heard the strident tones of Laurent's dam, demanding that her son's attacker be reprimanded since this was the practice ground. Well, if I was going to respond, it had to be before the instructors might intervene. I feinted left and then right. I repeated it, watching Laurent as he tried to work out what I was doing. It was a dance of sorts, intended to confuse the mind of the less agile. My dam came from Native Canadian stock and drum music was an integral part of what she had taught me. At the split second when Laurent's head following my movements was a fraction slow, I leapt, aiming for his hindquarters. My intention was not to take him down, but to show him that I was no easy target. It suited my dam and thus me, even as a pup, to not be the apple of Pierre Gosselin's eye. Let Laurent have that position, but even if he was acknowledged as the eldest and the heir, he would treat me with respect.

Laurent yelped as my teeth found their target. A quick bite down and release, the taste of his blood in my mouth, as I watched him limp slightly. I snarled again. My message was clear. That was a warning. Continue to play this game, and there will be one outcome. Back off now, and your pride will be intact. Laurent hesitated. I snarled and snapped at him again. Having scored first blood, I was deemed to have the upper hand. The voices of our instructors intruded, along with the whistle of one of the training staffs used to break up a fight as it swept between Laurent and me. With a final snarl, I shifted back to my human form, naked as the day I was born. That didn't matter. We were shifters. But, when Laurent shifted, the blood on his leg was there for all to see, just as the blood around my mouth was visible.

"Explain this!" The chief instructor knew that he would have to answer to Pierre Gosselin over why two of his get had been fighting. Everyone would know why we had fought. Dominance games, plain and simple. Neither Laurent nor I spoke. Neither of us wished to cede to the other. Allowing the instructors to separate us meant that, to an extent, the fight would be considered a draw. However, the important thing was that Laurent would know that I would fight back if he tried something similar again. If I had drawn blood on this instance, there was no telling what I might do the next time.

"Very well. The Alpha will be notified of the fight. It will be listed as a draw." The staff tapped us both, with enough force to leave a bruise on the arm struck. "The next unsanctioned fight will be taken to the natural conclusion." That meant that if we fought again, in this manner of one attacking the other without warning, then it would be a fight until one of us showed throat to the other. It would be a full dominance fight, in other words. I nodded my agreement, and walked to where my dam was standing. Her arms were folded, but the pride in her eyes was unmistakable, and there was just a hint of a smile on my own lips in response. Turning her back on me, she walked away, and I followed. After all, I was still a juvenile, and therefore, I was still obedient to her wishes.

The pup that I was knew that I might, but only might, have made a mistake, but something inside me knew that standing up to Laurent was important. I didn't know why, but I knew it was important. From the perspective of later in my life, I might suggest that it was because I would be recognised as his Beta-Designate. That might make me submissive to him, but I would be a poor Beta if I had surrendered too easily. But then, as a pup? I was making my point. I don't want to be a problem but I won't let you walk over me either.

<u>CHAPTER 5 - RECOGNITION</u>

So, two years after Pierre Gosselin ascended to the role of Alpha of the Gosselin Pack, he decided to recognise his three, male offspring: Laurent, Charles and me. Charles was a month younger than me, and, as was demonstrated recognised was as much so that I might not think my own position in the succession was a guaranteed thing. I am sure someone reading this will say that is an impossible thing for a six-year old to realise. But, we are not talking the world of humans here. A six-year old human is a child. A six-year old wolf is anything but a child, particularly in a pack like the Gosselin Pack that my sire seemed to think was the way forward.

One day I was living with my dam. The next, I was living in the Alpha's home, or rather in the home in which Janice Gosselin had spent her childhood and youth, before her mating. Again, in retrospect, so much is clearer. That is always the case. Then, what did I see? I saw my sire throw his mate across the hall, not caring how hard she hit the wall. He probably did care. He wanted it to hurt her. He wanted it to be clear that the word of Pierre Gosselin was law.

Laurent had stood there, watching, a smirk on his face at the sight of Janice Gosselin holding an arm up to protect her face from further blows. Our sire turned back to us, and there was a matching smirk on his face. My own face was expressionless. It had to be. I knew from my own dam that what I had just seen was wrong, but the only reason why I was here was because my own dam was dead, or so I believed. I had nowhere else to go. The old Alpha would never have done that to a female. There are dominance displays and there is brutality, and this was brutality.

"Instant obedience. That is what I expect." Pierre Gosselin did not look at Janice, but it was clear that the words were directed at her, and she knew it, nodding, as she pulled herself to her feet, using the wall for support.

"Come with me. Your rooms will be in the east wing." Janice's voice had been cold, but then even at six years old, I knew her options had been made clear: toe the line, the Pierre Gosselin line, or he would extract a penalty with his fists.

The 'east wing' was the opposite end of the house from the rooms she shared with Pierre Gosselin. Was it an attempt to protect us from the sound of her being 'disciplined' by her mate? Such questions were best not asked, just like it was best to pretend to not notice the bruises on her face, or the way she might cradle a bruised or sometimes broken arm.

Undoubtedly, Janice held no affection for the bastard get of her mate. We were there for one reason and one reason alone and that was to taunt her, to be a constant reminder of her failure to produce an heir of her bloodline. Of course, being thrown against a wall is hardly conducive to a female holding a pregnancy. But then, Pierre Gosselin had three male offspring, and if Janice were to succumb to her injuries, it would be his bloodline that would continue to rule the pack, unless she were to produce live young of her own.

CHAPTER 6 – THE NEW ORDER

As I have mentioned, when Pierre Gosselin finally assumed the title of Alpha, he had been mated to Janice for just over two years. Yes, our former Alpha, Janice's own sire, had shown more than just physical decline in his waning years and as a result the Gosselin Pack had lost some of its influence, not all, but certainly some.

There were several things that Pierre Gosselin had promised on mating Janice. The obvious one was to change his surname to Gosselin and thus ensure that any issue of their mating would bear the Gosselin name. So that was an immediate change. The other changes which Pierre Gosselin intended to make occurred in a more insidious manner, which given the sort of changes which they were, it was hardly surprising. Under the old Alpha for example, to wolves might mate for affection. Everybody knew that if the legends were to be believed at any rate, each of us had a mate, one who would form the other half of our souls. But finding that mate? That was the tricky part. So to wolves might be permitted to make for affection, since such a mating might equally produce pups. Under Pierre all that started to change. If the Gosselin Pack were to regain its level of influence, then his rule had to be obeyed. He was the only one who could return us to our former pre-eminence on the Shifter Council. For those who had lost money or other forms of wealth with the declining years of the former Alpha, the message spun by Pierre Gosselin made sense. They wanted the changes he might bring because it would mean that their own status would improve. But the problem was, that whilst such an approach might make sense to humans, we were not human. We were Pack. In theory, the petty needs of humans should not have concerned us. But in retrospect it could not be denied that one of the reasons why Pierre Gosselin could establish his rule was because he promised the sorts of measures that humans held dear: wealth and power over others.

What Pierre Gosselin suggested as the way forward was that Matings should be akin to the political alliances that used to be the norm amongst reigning families of England and Europe. It was, plain and simple, mating for power. The power was not necessarily for the young couple in question. No, the intention was in cementing such alliances that it was the Gosselin power that increased and more specifically, it was the power of Pierre Gosselin as the Alpha of the pack.

But changing how Matings were carried out was probably the least of the changes that Pierre Gosselin instigated. He said he wants to change the way that the pups were trained and prepared, so that they might contribute to the overall well-being of the pack. He would give rousing speeches on how we were Pack and how we should work together, both adults and pups. A benefit gained for the pack, he would say, was a benefit for all and likewise, anyone who caused the pack to lose, whether that was money or status, became a weakness that should be eliminated.

In my attempt to understand how Pierre Gosselin managed to hold sway over what was, after all, a very large pack, I have studied human history because when it came down to it, what my sire was doing was no different to any other dictator. He may have called himself the Alpha but he was little more than a dictator. Unfortunately by the time the rest of the pack realised what he was doing, it could be argued that it was too late.

The most chilling evidence of the changes that Pierre Gosselin made, and which the rest of the pack just seemed to accept was the fighting ring. He didn't call it the fighting ring to start with. It was an area for practice. It was an area the pack members to improve their skills. It was so we could all learn. It was so that the pack would benefit from the lessons that were learnt. Of course, by the time it was realised that the purpose of the fighting ring was to eliminate anyone whom Pierre Gosselin saw as a threat, it was too late. My sire was well and truly entrenched. He was truly the Alpha and his word was law. No one, and I mean no one, either dead or could countermand the changes that he made to the Gosselin Pack.

CHAPTER 7 – CHARLES

I had another sibling, a month younger than me, in Charles. Again, his dam had caught the eye of Pierre Gosselin during a full moon run. Two months later, Charles had been born. He was not as strong a pup physically as either Laurent or I, but he made up for it with brains. He appreciated tactics, alliances and that was how he maintained his own rank amongst the younglings. He was still the get of Pierre Gosselin and whilst his dam may not have been as vocal as Laurent's dam, she had made it clear who had sired her pup.

How did I view Charles? Did I see him as a threat to me? Physically, no, he was no threat. For me, the threat lay with Laurent and his little coterie of followers. It could be said that Charles and I became allies. Tactics. We could not be seen to be building a rival 'court' to Laurent. Such an obvious move would have meant painting a giant target across our own backs. Laurent and his little gang would act and it would be messy.

Does that mean to say that I feared what Laurent would do? I was six years old when I arrived in Janice Gosselin's house. To say that I was scared is perhaps to use the wrong word. I was not scared because my dam had explained to me that this was my right. I was sired by Pierre Gosselin. I was his son whether or not at the time Janice wished to acknowledge that. For that matter I was as much Pierre's son as Laurent, again regardless of whether he wished to acknowledge it. Could the same be said of Charles? The key difference between Laurent and Charles was that Laurent's dam had willingly born a child to Pierre Gosselin. On the other hand, Charles's dam had been raped. She had not wish to associate with Pierre Gosselin believing that the vows he had spoken with Janice should have some degree of being sacred. But she failed to appreciate the sort of male that was Pierre Gosselin. If he wished to take something, he would take it. That was the plain and simple truth. So how did this affect Charles and his standing amongst the three of us? Charles was not a leader. He did not wish to lead. Given the choice particularly as he grew older, I suspect that Charles would have been quite happy to sink back into anonymity. But that was not his choice to make.

Whether he wanted it or not Charles served another purpose. And that purpose was to remind me Casimir, that I could be replaced. Second son I might be. Theoretical heir to Laurent I might be. But, because Charles existed, I was replaceable.

It was dinner one evening, when Pierre Gosselin put into words what I suspected in terms of Charles' role. Our sire was in an expansive mood. A property deal had been particularly advantageous, adding to both the physical and financial wealth of the Gosselin Pack. Our sire was a powerfully built male. He had made it his habit to have a formal dinner, to which he would invite those in favour with him, or those who sought his favour. Janice Gosselin would be the gracious hostess, any bruises hidden under carefully applied makeup. Laurent, Charles and I would be dressed in miniature copies of our sire's garments, the clear evidence of his strength as an Alpha. On this evening, it was just 'family', and, sitting opposite us, three of the group of adult males who were viewed as the Alpha's assistants. Enforcers, by any other name.

Leaning back in his chair at the end of the meal, our sire toyed with a cigar. He used to play with them, rolling them between his fingers, never smoking them, but just playing with it, a sign of his wealth. He had looked at the three adult males, a smile on his face, before gesturing towards the three of us. His three sons. Proof positive of his virility.

"I have made a decision." He announced. "I have three sons. Laurent, your role has been made clear as my eldest. You are the Alpha Designate." He gestured to the enforcer sitting opposite my sibling. "Arnaud will take your training in hand, so that you understand the mindset required to be a strong

Alpha." His gaze fell on me. "Casimir, as my second son, your role will be that of Beta Designate. You will be Beta to your elder brother's Alpha in due course. Matthieu will be your mentor."

Charles shrank back in his chair as our sire turned to him. The remaining of the three enforcers had a smirk on his face. "And you, Charles." The cigar twirled in his fingers, and he, too, had a smirk on his face. "Third son, but already demonstrating that you are not as ... forthcoming as your brothers." He picked up the cut-crystal glass of whisky at his side, and took a thoughtful sip, his eyes never leaving Charles. "You serve a very specific purpose. Your brother, Casimir, as well as being Beta Designate, is also my 'spare', should anything happen to Laurent. You, Charles, serve the same purpose. Should Casimir not be up to scratch, you will replace him in rank." His eyes swung back to me. "No one is irreplaceable, Casimir. Just remember that."

His gaze landed on each of us in turn, before he looked at the three enforcers. "Arnaud, Matthieu and Jean will act as your mentors. You will follow their instructions during physical training. Failure to do so will be reported to me, and I will decide on appropriate action if merited by your transgression." He smiled, taking another sip from his whisky glass. "Are we clear, gentlemen?"

We might only have been children, none of us yet ten years old, but we knew exactly what he meant. The three enforcers were not known for their gentle touch. Their lessons would not be easy. Whilst I would have my ... day of reckoning with Mathieu, the same was unlikely for Charles.

Without a doubt, as we grew up in the home of Janice Gosselin, Charles had it made only too clear that his only purpose was to remind me that I was replaceable. As for any involvement in our sire's activities, forget whether Charles agreed with those activities. Or rather, let me make it clear. Charles did not agree with those activities. However, he lacked the sense to keep those opinions to himself and as my brothers and I grew, that lack of discretion would be Charles's downfall.

CHAPTER 8 – CHARLES VS LAURENT

Whilst Charles and I might have had a reasonably amicable relationship, the same could not be said of Charles and Laurent. As I have said Laurent was a bully even when we were young pups, even before we were recognised as the sons of Pierre Gosselin, Laurent wish to make it clear that he was the eldest, he was the one likely to succeed our sire. To make that even clearer to us, should it have been necessary, even as a pup Laurent was prepared to use his fists. Not so much on me, but on Charles? Most definitely.

Janice had assigned us all quarters in the east wing of the Alpha's home. Each of us had our own suites, since after all we were the sons of the Alpha. Of course, Laurent's suite was the largest. That is not to say that mine was a small room, since for me, it was more than adequate. Equally, the room that was assigned to Charles, our youngest sibling amongst the bastard offspring of Pierre Gosselin, was not an inconsiderable size. But, and Laurent made a point of emphasising this on a regular basis, his rooms with the biggest and the most luxurious.

Charles was probably the most studious of three of us. I suspect that of the three of us he was the least like our sire and more like his own dam. That was unfortunate for him. As I said, Charles was born the product of rape. His dam never really recovered from what had happened to her. The only reason, or at least the only reason many suspected, that Charles was recognised as a son of Pierre Gosselin, was that he did bear a remarkable resemblance to his sire, perhaps even more so than Laurent or I. But that resemblance, that caused its own problems.

Laurent above all wanted to prove and wanted everyone to remember, that he was the eldest. He wanted everyone to acknowledge, at all times, that he would be the Alpha after his sire. The fact that Charles for a greater resemblance to our sire than his alleged primary heir did not sit well with Laurent. As studious as Charles might be, he could not help but be aware of Laurent's animosity towards him. So yes, it was inevitable, that there would be a confrontation, and it would be a very physical confrontation. Unlike Laurent fight with me, the only outcome that would result in Charles not losing his life would be the him to show throat to Laurent. Failure to admit to Laurent's dominance over him, even when Laurent was still a juvenile, would have meant Charles's death regardless of the consequences.

Lest it appear that Laurent was shall we say all brawn and no brain, I should make it clear that he did have some intelligence. In the case of his dominance fight with Charles, that intelligence demonstrated itself in the understanding that the confrontation must take place away from adult eyes. To make the impression that Laurent sought on his youngest brother, he had to make Charles fearful of going to an adult. So in retrospect it is somewhat ironic that I was the one whom people would call the Psycho.

Laurent had waited until winter to make his move. The Gosselin territory included the Laurentian Mountains. I wondered sometimes if my brother thought that the similarity of the ranges name to his own made it some sort of "special playground" where he might perpetrate his idea of games. That's enough philosophy. What Laurent did know, is that whilst Charles was able to scrape through the requirements for winter survival, skills which we were all taught, he did not excel in those skills. He knew enough to keep himself alive, and if necessary, he could manage minor injuries. Anything more than that, and Charles might have been in considerable trouble.

Laurent's intention in waylaying Charles in the mountains, was to ensure that his younger brother was at a disadvantage. As far as Laurent was concerned the fight might well end with Charles being injured to the point where his survival questionable. When I became aware of what Laurent intended to do, I was faced with two choices. I could either cement my own position as the second son and likely beta to my older brothers Alpha when the time came, or I could pit myself against not just Laurent but his coterie of friends. Make no mistake, to opt for the latter course of action, could mean that I was putting my own life at risk. Was I prepared to do that? Would it not been easier for me to say, if Charles is being used as a constant reminder to me that my position exists purely at the whim of my sire, if I allowed Laurent to have his fun, then I was serving myself. I would make sure that my position was inviolate, because there was no third son. If Charles died, at least until Janice produced offspring of her own, then all Pierre Gosselin had to show with the two of us.

That, would have been such an easy course of action.

I didn't take it.

There was a way that I could compromise, and that was to use what I knew of Laurent's plan against Charles. Bear in mind that as the sons of Pierre Gosselin each of us bore his stamp. Laurent's plan was some time in the execution, because what he had to do was first convince his younger sibling that he wanted nothing more than sibling bonding. Humans have a phrase, a cliché, in that if something looks too good to be true, then it probably is. With hindsight, that is how Charles should have viewed Laurent's approach to him. But to use another human cliché, everyone has the benefit of 20/20 vision with hindsight. Had we been adults, Laurent's plan would never have succeeded, because it was too simplistic. But at the time we were but pups, and that was something that Laurent used to his advantage. Of course, pups play. Of course, their games can be a little rough. Surely that was all that was happening? A little rough housing, that was all? If anything, it could be argued, that in taking his youngest sibling under his wing as Laurent wished it to appear, he was being the soul of helpfulness. Again, let me insert a human phrase. I believe the term is pass me the sick bag. As Laurent grew older yes it was apparent that he did nothing that did not benefit him and him alone. But as pups, people believed him, and they believed that all he was doing, along with his friends, was puppy play fighting. That was all. No harm intended. It was only play.

However, there is never only play when you are talking the Laurentian Mountains and winter.

Even as a pup I remember that full moon runs as a pack in winter was something to be enjoyed, something to be relished. By and large, the pack would run over territory which was untouched by human intrusion. We would not play on their marked ski runs, not even the so-called black runs. Where is the pleasure to be found in running on such open country? No, the pleasure is in weaving through the trees as they stood silent sentinels, their branches heavy with snow. There, high up in the mountains, a sound wrong time might bring that snow, not just from the trees but also from the hillsides, crashing down, trapping those foolish enough or unwary. This was all part of our winter survival training. Both as pups and our human forms, we had to know how to survive should we be trapped in an avalanche. Let's face it, if you did not master the skills there was only one likely outcome. Death.

But it did not suit Laurent's purpose to kill Charles, at least not at that stage. Even though we had not been recognised by our sire as his blooded offspring, there were rumours but this was inevitable. Two years after being mated to Pierre Gosselin and Janice had yet to produce a child of her own. Of course the cynic might say that she stood a better chance of holding a pregnancy if her mate did not use his fists on her. But no one wish to bring attention, or shame, on the daughter of the former Alpha, not then, not when her mating was still relatively new. That would change later but a scant two years into her mating to Pierre Gosselin, nobody mentioned what was becoming more and more apparent.

So, a full moon run and as I have said, it should have been a time to enjoy. But Charles is enjoyment of that full moon run would be forever tainted by the actions of Laurent and his little gang. The upshot was that Charles was buried in the snow. But, and this was key, Laurent and his gang had forced him to shift from his wolf form back to human and had then engineered the snowfall which had buried him. Understand that this meant Charles was naked and human. Unlike wolves humans are somewhat lacking when it comes to survival of cold temperatures. The irony of how Charles nearly died is not lost on me now, but I skip ahead of myself. I had been watching, waiting for Laurent to make his move. How I knew he would make his move that night I do not know but I had my suspicions. The question will always remain whether Laurent expected Charles to survive. But courtesy of my intervention, he did. He had only been buried scant minutes when I had dug him free. He was barely conscious so still in my own wolf form I had lain next to him, sharing the considerably higher body temperature of a wolf with his shivering form. When he had stopped shivering sufficiently to be able to concentrate, Charles shifted back to his own wolf form. But both of us knew what Laurent intended Charles to know: your life is in my hands.

In effect, it meant that Charles only role was to keep me in line, and to remind me that I was replaceable. I wonder now whether as I proved my importance and my usefulness to my sire, did that play a role in Charles's eventual demise? That I don't know.

CHAPTER 9 – THE GOSSELIN PRINCESS

I was eight years old when Janice managed finally to produce an heir of her body, not that the pup would have a chance at the succession. And, that was not because it was a female pup, my sister Alix. Nothing, and I mean nothing would be permitted to supplant Laurent.

The rumour was that Janice went into seclusion in the latter part of her pregnancy due to modesty, of not wishing to appear in public with an 'unsightly' pregnant belly. The truth was another demonstration of my sire's delicate touch. Facial bruises were only part of it. The reason that Janice had quartered Laurent, Charles and me in the east wing was so that we didn't discover the reality of her mating. Mated because she thought she loved her mate, she discovered to her cost that he loved one thing only: power. He wanted to be Alpha, and if that meant putting up with a mewling bitch like Janice, as I heard him say, then so be it.

On the day that she was brought to childbed with Alix, she was nursing a broken arm, and yet, she refused to scream. She did not wish her child to hear its dam screaming, even if it was in the birthing process. Later, she would tell me that she screamed enough during her mating. This was one occasion when she would remain silent.

However, even if the pup could not be in the line of succession, it was still required that the birth be witnessed so there was no doubt that the pup was from Janice's line. This was critical, because my sire had another delightful habit. Female pups were not permitted to live. There was enough 'breeding stock' as he referred to them. So, witnesses had to be those whom he could be certain would not mention his orders. If the pup was female, then he intended it did not leave the room alive.

The birth was quick, which was something for Janice at least. The midwife had cleaned the pup, and examined it. I had seen her hands shake as she looked at my sire.

"It is a female." She whispered, knowing what would follow. She may not agree with the 'policy', but she also valued her own life.

Pierre Gosselin had grabbed the newborn female pup from the midwife. Janice had made a mewl of fear for her newborn but with a broken arm she was powerless to stop her mate. I can still recall the look on my sire's face. It had been a cold look, gloating, because he knew that Janice was powerless against him. In retrospect one might ask what kind of male took such pleasure in seeing such a look of fear on the face of his mate. Without a doubt for me, this was a defining moment. Even at the age of eight years old I knew this to be a defining moment. Was this part of my bloodline coming to the fore? I didn't know, not that age. But what I did know, was that the look on my sire's face was almost indecent in its pleasure. The wailing baby had hung over her dam's bed as those present had looked on. We all knew that it was Pierre Gosselin's habit to kill any female offspring. There were no exceptions, not even a pup whom he himself had sired. That is what should have been the fate of this newborn female pup. My sire would claim that only a small number of breeding females were necessary in the pack. That was the only purpose of females, to produce more males. He wanted strong males. The feeble had no place in his vision of the Gosselin Pack.

I don't know why I spoke up at that point, but I did. After all what was I, but an eight-year-old pup, the second born, even if I had been acknowledged as one of his heirs. Laurent had looked at me as I spoke. He had that smirk, and almost perpetual expression on his face, partially hopeful that in speaking I might bring the wrath of my sire upon my head, and thus give Laurent an excuse to reprimand me, even if he was a scant year older than me, because he was the heir to the Alpha of the Gosselin Pack. But I had spoken nonetheless.

"Sir, may I suggest an alternative idea?" Whilst my voice was still unbroken, I had recently started making a name for myself in the hand to hand combat lessons that was part of our training. Such lessons meant that physically, I looked more than a child of eight years. I was conscious of Janice's eyes on me, and the fact that the room was quiet. Even the newborn child was only making whimpering noises, no doubt at the cool temperature of the room. "This female pup is the first offspring of your mate. There are those who would say that she is the heir over Laurent. Would it not be better to hold her life in your hands in return for their continued loyalty to your true heir?"

Apart from the whimpering of the newborn pup, my sister Alix, there was no sound in the room as my sire considered my suggestion. All eyes were on him. No one dared glance at me unless you counted Laurent and his periodic smirk in my direction, almost as if he was hoping that our sire would agree that I had crossed the line. But there was a key issue. There were two things to note here. The first was that my sire liked to think that he held the pack in a fist of iron, but the truth was not that. It had only been two years or perhaps a little bit longer than that since he had taken over control and he had started to instigate the various changes which would ensure that he might rule by fear. So anything which might strengthen his position was likely to meet with his approval. That was the reason I made my suggestion, phrasing it the way that I had. He knew that the plan was sound. A glance at Janice and then another at the room around us. He nodded. "The idea is sound. The female pup may live."

Swiftly, the midwife wrapped the infant in a blanket and passed her to Janice, who put Alix to her breast immediately. Reassured by the child's suckling, Janice seemed to relax, but I knew that she was watching me. Yes, I had suggested that my sire could use the pup to control her, but and this was key, I had also saved the life of her firstborn. I knew when I met her gaze fleetingly, that she would not forget what I had done. Thus began "the great pretence", the plan which Janice and I were to develop over time which would serve to protect not just my new sister Alix, but the rest of the pack, even though I knew that it was not my pack to rule. And more to the point it would never be my pack to rule.

CHAPTER 10 – ALIX AND ADHÉMAR

Janice's second child was born six months later, the product of rape by her own mate. This time, no distance would have prevented my brothers and me from hearing her screams. She had come to visit her daughter in the nursery to feed her. However, our sire had guests from the Shifter Council and at the end of the evening, an evening from which his mate had absented herself, he had stormed into the nursery, where Janice had just laid Alix down. Throwing his Mate backwards against the wall, he had 'explained' with his fists what he thought of the way he had been embarrassed in front of the Shifter Council. And then he had raped her.

No one came to Janice's aid. No one dared to come to Janice's aid and it is to my shame that I include myself in that number. Perhaps you might say that I should have, consequences be damned. But, even though I had demonstrated some prowess in the training programme instigated by my sire, I was still physically a pup of under nine years. My sire was an adult full-grown. At that point, had I gone to Janice's assistance there would have been one conclusion. I would have died that night. There are those, again with the benefit of hindsight, who would say better that you had died that night, doing something that was vaguely good, then you lived to perpetrate the evil that made you the Psycho Gosselin. But as I said at the start of this commentary, all I ask is that you read to the end of what I have to say. Do not judge me for my actions until you know the full story. To rape anyone, whether male or female, is a heinous crime by any species standard. And when the rape is carried out by the pack Alpha, whose responsibility it should be to protect his pack members, then that crime is magnified. Psycho Gosselin I might have been called but it was never said that I committed rape.

Janice fell pregnant with Adhémar as a result. Now my sire had a new target. A male pup, and one who, if he lived, could be used as a candidate against Laurent, since he was a blooded Gosselin. If he lived. That was the key point: if he lived. Accidents happen in childhood and it seemed that more often than not, it was Adhémar who would bear the brunt of such 'accidents'.

Adhémar was born within a similar setup to Alix. Everything, right down to the fact that Janice was nursing another broken arm. Given my role in preventing Alix from being killed at birth, along with the fact that I was the 'second son', I was present amongst the witnesses. Again, Janice refused to scream, even though her face had been pale as she struggled to bring Adhémar into the world. With her broken arm, she couldn't grip the headboard of the bed to try to relieve the pain. When the pup was born, again, the midwife had cleaned him quickly. Everyone had expected that Janice would again bear a female. She did herself. But then came the midwife's words: "It is a male."

I don't know who gasped, but someone in the room did, because we all knew the implications of Janice bearing a male. This was a blooded male Gosselin. Not a Gosselin by adoption of the name, but a blooded descendant of the Alpha before Pierre Gosselin. If there had not been witnesses in the room, Adhémar's life might have ended then and there. Interestingly, my sire had looked at me. My face bore its habitual cold expression, a look I had taken pains to cultivate. Cold indifference was my own protection. No emotion. Again, it served a purpose.

"Well, Casimir, do you see a use for a male pup?" Pierre had sneered at Janice as he spoke.

"Even more so that with the female pup … sir." I had replied. "If a female pup might be used to force others to accept Laurent as your heir, then having the male pup under your control means that you have all the 'aces' so to speak."

"Interesting point, whelp." My sire looked thoughtful. "Very well, the pup lives. Give him to his dam." The midwife hurried to carry out his instructions, and again, Janice held her pup to her breast, heavy as they were with milk, particularly now that she had two pups to feed. Her expression had softened as she watched her pup feed, such that it wasn't until Pierre's hand curved around her face, forcing her to look at him, that her expression changed to its more usual cross between defensive and fearful. "I chose to let your pup live, but equally, I can choose to have him put down. Don't forget that, my mate." He had laughed at the sudden fear in Janice's eyes. The softened expression was gone, replaced with the more familiar pallor and dilated eyes. Grinning, Pierre had slapped her cheek, probably with more force than was necessary, before leaving the room. Without a word, Laurent and I followed him.

The sound of my sire attacking Janice had stirred something within me. It was wrong. Not even past puberty myself but I knew I could not tolerate what was happening before me. As everyone filed out of Janice's room, I paused. My sire had looked back at me a questioning look on his face.

"To understand the weakness of a target one must study it." I commented looking directly at Janice as she sat nursing her child. "If I may, sir, I wish to engage in such study." Such words from the mouth of a pup not yet nine years old, such cold hard words. I made it sound as if Janice and the infant Adhémar were little more than a laboratory experiment to me. My tone said that they may well have been a bacteria sample in a petri dish for all the importance that I put by them. But if the germ of an idea that was forming in my head had a chance of success, my sire had to believe the image before him. He had to believe that I was little more than a cold-hearted, and emotionless psychopath in the making.

How the truth differed from the reality. Janice and I made a pact, but it was a long term plan. Adhémar would be the next Alpha of the Gosselin Pack, but he had to reach adulthood, and he had to be prepared to fight. So, a slightly built male, who took after his dam, didn't have a childhood, because I had to ensure that he learned and learned quickly. He had to be able to fight in ways that were unexpected if he was to overcome the physically bigger Laurent. I became adept at being on hand when my sire felt that our youngest sibling needed to learn a lesson, or when he had to face the aftermath of Laurent's idea of 'teaching'. It was incredible that Adhémar did not suffer from the number of broken bones or the times his nose was broken. My gut instinct told me that it was vitally important that my sibling retained his distinctive appearance. It was ironic indeed when the reason for that came to pass. However, that is of no consequence here.

There was one effect of my pact with Janice that was interesting. My sire seemed to think that he could use my ability to fight to his advantage. He was already using an interesting talent I was developing: the ability to spot business trends which were sources of significant profit. The wealth of Gosselin Pack increased apace, but then came the day that my sire chose to not follow my suggestion. Whilst it was not a catastrophic loss on the markets, it was a considerable dent in the financial situation. Rather than accept the blame for his own mistake, my sire decided that I must face 'trial' in the fighting ring. This was a little delight that he had instigated to 'train' the younger members of the pack, and occasionally their parents, in the fighting skills which he deemed essential had become much more in just a matter of months. It was a thinly veiled excuse for his coterie of bodyguards to beat the living shit out of anyone who crossed Pierre Gosselin. Death was often the result, or at the very best, disabling injuries. On the day that it was announced that I would face an adult opponent in the fighting ring as a penalty for the shame and the financial loss I brought upon the pack, I was twelve years old.

<u>CHAPTER 11 – FIRST FIGHT</u>

The fighting ring was outside. Overhung by trees a stranger looking at it, and by a stranger I mean a non-wolf shifter, might think that it was a corral of some kind. After all, not far from the house with the stables in which the immediate members of the Gosselin family kept their chosen horses. And the truth was it did look a lot like an outdoor riding school with its split rail fencing and sanded surface. My sire thought it amusing to emphasise the effect by having various pieces of equine harness hanging from the posts. But this was no riding school. By the time I was twelve years old the fighting ring had another name. The name that the members of the pack would whisper to themselves was the Ring of Death.

The sanded surface made it easier to soak up the blood. After all, a quick raking and the ring would be ready for the next bout. The fights were always bare-fisted, and the opponents bare-chested. Some packs held such fights in wolf form only, but my sire preferred us to fight in our 'weaker' forms of human. It would make us more resilient and able to uphold the 'honour' of the Gosselin pack.

Twelve years old, and I was to face an adult opponent in the fighting ring because my sire chose not to follow my 'gut feeling' and the pack lost money. More to the point, his twelve-year-old whelp made him lose face and for that, I must pay. My sire liked to give the impression that he was in complete control of the Gosselin Pack and to this end maintaining face was very important to him. When visitors would come from the shifter Council, he wanted them to see Pierre Gosselin, the Alpha, the ruler of the Gosselin financial and territorial empire. What had I done, when I had "lost" money for the pack? Since it was known that my sire followed my advice, if the Pack had lost money, it must mean that I had given my sire bad advice. Therefore it was only reasonable that I was the one who had to pay.

It was not I who paid. To this day, the pack talks about that fight, what it was rumoured some saw. At the time, I could not have explained what happened. I may have been a mere boy, but I was also a wolf shifter, and I was a keen sportsman. It showed in my physique. My abilities in hand-to-hand combat training had been noted, and that why I faced a very specific opponent.

The physical contrast between my opponent and me could not have been greater. I was twelve years old. Yes, I may have been fighting in the practice ring for the last four years, but I was still a pup, bordering on puberty. My opponent was an adult full-grown. As was the case with several of my sire's enforcers, Matthieu was heavily muscled. His fists showed how much he liked to use them. His nose had been broken several times and he wore it like some sort of macabre badge. As I entered the ring, I knew that others would also note the contrast in our physiques. Even though I had a reputation for being cold, I would like to think that others had noted that fight was not "fair". But then again in the years that Pierre Gosselin had ruled this pack, fair was not a term used often. Whilst we were both bare-chested and bare fisted for this fight, I had also chosen to fight barefoot. I wore a pair of karate gi trousers. Strangely enough it didn't seem to matter that the trousers would probably be ruined. Blood would fly during this encounter. If anything was certain it was that. Since the likely outcome of this fight was that I would die, who would care if one pair of karate gi trousers were ruined.

I suppose one question is whether I felt myself that I was going to my death that morning? When I think back, to what was going through my mind, it was the fact that I was twelve years old. Had I been a human child, at the age of twelve years old, I would be thinking attending middle school or perhaps football practice or considering that I lived in Canada ice hockey practice. I might be considering a girl whom I thought cute or I might be considering all manner of things that human children consider. I'm a wolf. How would I know what human children consider important at the age of twelve? So, an answer to that question of whether I thought that I would die that day? Yes. I did think that my chances of living were extremely slim but equally I had something to spur me on to win.

Just under four years had passed since Janice and I had agreed our pact. I had something to live for as I walked into that ring that particular morning, because even in four years one thing had become apparent. I had to live. I had to survive. It was not just about me, not any more. It had not been just about me for the last four years. It was about Alix, it was about Adhémar. It was about Janice. It was about the Gosselin Pack that had existed before my sire had taken the reins. twelve years old and so many depended on me already? Janice had taken a huge risk. She had taken the chance that my actions which had served to save the lives of both of her new-borns were an indication that I was potentially an ally. It would have been all too easy for me to report her approaches to me to my sire. To do so would have meant not just Janice's death but Alix's death and Adhémar's death. And make no mistake the plan that Janice and I was slowly building would have one endpoint only. Pierre Gosselin would die.

To attribute the success of such a plan to a mere twelve-year-old seemed strange. Surely I must be giving myself an overinflated opinion of my importance, surely? In many ways I wish I was over estimating my importance. But the unfortunate thing was that it wasn't so much that I was important, it was the fact that at that point, when my sire held sway, when he had his band of enforcers, when he used such things as the fight ring to instil fear in those Pack members who might still try to stand against him, there were few others who might stand against him in truth. And I was twelve years old.

How was the fight described? My speed was noted. The way that my opponent reeled back as I struck blow after blow, punches, kicks, a rapid fire of attack became part of pack stories. They spoke of how my whole demeanour seemed to change. Some said they saw my eyes change for the first time, or at least the first time in the fighting ring. Adhémar would tell me afterwards that when we would have our 'sessions', both he and Alix had noticed how my eyes changed from their usual blue to a darker shade, almost a black iris surrounding the pupil. The blood on the sand that day was mine, but it was more that of my opponent.

When the fight was ended, I had one knee on my opponent's back, my fist was in his hair, pulling his head up and back as he gasped for breath, the blood dripping from his nose and mouth. His swollen eyes had looked at my sire, and he had known what the outcome would be, even as I made it clear where I could take this fight. This was one of my father's 'enforcers', who relished being able to maintain pack discipline. And he was on the verge of death at the hands of a pup.

My sire had nodded and a blade had landed within my reach. Grabbing it with my free hand, I had forced my opponent's head higher, exposing his neck. The blood fountained from the slash. Something inside me changed that day, almost as if another part of a jigsaw puzzle was made to fit. When I stood, the leather handle of a bloodied blade clenched in my fist, I had looked at my sire, only at him. I had inclined my head in the barest of nods, and turned, leaving the ring without a word.

That had been just the first of many bouts. Perhaps my sire wished to prove that the first bout had been a fluke, a mere lucky chance for me, a bad day for my opponent. Bad day was an understatement. Something had changed that day, the start of a reputation which I was to develop, and I was a pup barely out of puberty.

In closing this particular chapter there is one thing I should point out. I mentioned that it felt as if something had changed that day. Well the truth was something did change. I did something that day which, as I was to discover later, really did change something within me. For the first time, I spilled the blood of another with deliberate purpose. Whilst I may not have dedicated that blood in the way dictated by my bloodline, the fact remains that the spilling of blood on that sanded surface counted as a key element of who I am. When it became known from where my dam's family had originated, so much would become clear. But, after that first fight, after that first kill, all of that was unknown to me. All I knew was that something had changed and as I looked at my sire, as I gave him that slightest of nods and as I ignored my brother Laurent, much to his dismay, I had what the implications of those actions might mean in the long-term. Truth be told, all I want to do at that point was to lose the bloodstained karate gi trousers, to have a shower and to sleep. As the saying goes, if wishes were fishes, there would be no hunger in the world of man. If wishes were fishes.

CHAPTER 12 – NOT A FLUKE

My sire's iron hold on the pack was to grow tighter.
Infractions which he may have permitted in the early days
brought down his full wrath on the transgressors. Where was
the Shifter Council in all this? Where indeed? What about the
mythical 'judge, jury and executioner', the legendary Cŵn
Annwn? Well, clearly they were nothing more than a myth. I
did remember my dam telling me stories of these creatures
who acted as the soldiers of the Goddess, acted as the final
justice, reading the souls of the accused in order to judge
whether they were innocent or guilty. And if they were found
guilty then there was one outcome only: death. The sole
would be "harvested". They also was supposed to serve a
purpose in protecting the innocent and as things started to
change in the Gosselin Pack, their lack of intervention was
seen in the despair, as others, likewise brought up on those
legends, began to realise or to believe at least that those
legends were just stories. No one would come to their
assistance.

A question asked often throughout history is how a dictator
gains their power. After all it is one individual. Just one. Even
if they have a coterie of followers, of lieutenants, they are still
only one individual, so how does it work. The answer is
always the same. It is a combination of apathy and of the
despair that comes with the knowledge that to attempt to fight
serves no purpose other than to bring death upon oneself. So
think if you will, of a male, of an adult, who knows
instinctively that what they are seeing is wrong, but if they
fight, they will die. Who will protect their dependents then?
Better surely, that one bows one's head to the dictator and
accepts the new status quo. Thus do dictators hold sway. Thus
my sire strengthened his hold on the Gosselin Pack.

The fact was that the Gosselin Pack had increased both its financial wealth and its level of influence under my sire. Pierre Gosselin was seen as a force within Shifter Council politics. What did it matter if he was heard to be scornful of those not 'gifted' with shifter ability? We were paranormal creatures. We had every right to hold ourselves above humans, the pond scum that they were. They were too ignorant to even realise the 'beasts' that walked amongst them. His coterie of followers and those bodyguards who had been loyal to him reaped the benefits of that loyalty in terms of wealth and influence. Rumours abounded of some of my sire's business interests, which skated close to the line of legality. But what did he care? There was always a fall guy, always someone else. He was using my own abilities in identifying market trends more and more, but he was also using me as an enforcer. Did I enjoy the latter? No. Categorically no. But there was an undercurrent in the Pack.

Broken bones did ensue from my enforcement of my sire's orders, with a severity of injury sufficient that my sire felt I was fulfilling my role as his enforcer, but shifters heal, and they can heal faster than humans. If I saw, or noticed, the vague stirrings of hope on someone's face that their punishment would be from my hands rather than from Laurent or one of my sire's enforcers, I had to ignore it. If anything I had to cultivate the look that caused people to whisper that I was a psychopath. I had to cultivate a look that said I enjoyed the tears, and I enjoyed the pain that I inflicted. If anything a small part of me died each time I had to administer those very public punishments. But if I did not, the options were limited. I developed a pattern whereby my sire was assured that punishments I carried out in private away from others were of a suitable severity that both the recipient and their family would know that a lesson was being served. Had that duty fall into one of my sire's lieutenants, the punishment would have been carried out in public. Instead of a beating when I used my fists, it might be a public flogging, which would leave the recipient with a shredded back and with not just physical scars, but mental scars.

The first time an adult female had laid her hand on my arm after I had administered a punishment and I saw the mute thanks in her eyes that the only result was a broken arm and very colourful but surface injuries on her mate, I realised that I was playing a very dangerous game.

"Say nothing." I had hissed at her. "I neither want nor need your thanks. Your mate was foolish to draw the Alpha's attention to his actions and must pay the price."

The female had nodded. She had already dosed her mate with a sedative. Without a word, I had laid a hand on the bandaged arm and I felt something, akin to an electric shock or a burst of static. The somnolent male had jerked before settling again. After that incident, it became something of a habit for me, that a similar touch whilst it would not heal the injuries it would make them less of a problem.

Two more of his enforcers died in the fighting ring at my hands, each death more brutal that before. Those deaths I did enjoy, not least since one of them was Charles' assigned 'mentor', Jean. It was not just that they were enforcing my sire's will but they enjoyed causing pain and they enjoyed seeing the fear in their victim's eyes. What they failed to realise was that others would jockey for their positions and others would cause them to fall from favour. And each time that I brought more wealth to the pack through my dabbling in the stock markets, my sire would grant me a reward. If he saw my enjoyment in killing these individuals, he thought only that it strengthened his hold on me, because I had no doubt that each and every one of those deaths was recorded somewhere, a hidden threat to be used against me should I ever step out of line. But, then to my mind, they had been longer 'in post', with more blood of their own pack mates on their hands. An eye for an eye to my mind. Their eyes for taking the lives of others.

What if those I disciplined was seen to heal rapidly? My questions not be asked? Might the accusation not be made that perhaps I was not administering the punishment that my sire felt was appropriate? Yes, that was always going to be a risk. Perhaps that was why, when I would touch those injuries, whatever happened, that burst of static, all that it served to do was to bring the injury to a point when the victim's own body could heal it. That way it could not be said that I was going easy on them. My sire said that it was another sign of the strength of the Gosselin Pack: that even those with injuries healed quickly. Was it? I don't know, and in the ensuing four years since that first fight, I was as concerned with any other member of the Gosselin Pack in ensuring that I remained alive, with no time to ruminate over the rapid healing abilities of my 'victims'.

CHAPTER 13: CHARLES' DECISION

In the end it was the actions of my brother, Charles, which serve to set my reputation as the Psycho Gosselin. For that both I and my pack mates owe him a debt. He allowed himself to be a sacrifice. He had reached the decision that the loss of his own life would serve a greater purpose than trying to appease our sire. In making that sacrifice, he saved lives. It is as simple as that. Yet it started with little more than a conversation between two brothers on a cold, winter's night.

"Casimir." The barest pause in the grooming of my assigned stallion was the only indication that I heard Charles' whisper. He appeared on the other side of the stallion, another brush in his hands. Two brothers, working together. Nothing suspicious there. "Cas, I am to face trial in the fighting ring."

The stallion snorted, stamping a hoof impatiently, his breath making clouds of steam in the cool night air. It was winter. Snow was on the ground and in theory the pack was preparing public celebrations of the Christmas break. Nothing beat playing happy families, did it?

"I know you said I should not countermand his orders on the new business venture." Charles continued to brush the already shining coat of the stallion, his voice barely a whisper. "Well, I guess I am to pay the price."

"It won't be me. It seems my usual opponents are behaving." My voice held more than a hint of sarcasm. Others had taken note of the usual outcome if I fought in the ring. I was the ultimate deterrent, the way that our sire ensured the compliant behaviour of others.

"Cas, I don't want to die like that." Charles paused in his work. "I know I fucked up, but I will not be a part of what he is doing, using human females like that. He calls it farming now, as if they are little more than livestock."

"You think that I am any more enthralled by the situation. I don't have the choice of acting for myself, and you fucking know that, brother." For all my vehemence, my voice was as quiet. It would not do for our conversation to be overheard. I would ensure this particular venture of our sire's was as short lived as possible, but for now, I could do little. Legally, I was still a minor, and thus under his control.

"I need your help, brother. I will take my own life, but I need your help." For a moment, Charles rested his head on the gleaming coat of the stallion. Looking up, there was a quiet resolution on my brother's face. "If the plan I have in mind works out, it will benefit not just the two of us, but others also. Your reputation as a killer will be inviolate. No one will dare to cross you, and you will be able to continue to … do what you do."

"Carry on." I took up one of the stallions legs between my own, checking the hoof for stones, and ensuring that the shoe did not need replacing.

"You are acknowledged as one of the experts in winter survival. I need to do my refresher course." Charles had clearly given this plan some considerable thought. "How familiar are you with the treatment protocols for hypothermia in the mountains?" Again, he looked at me. "The Laurentian Mountains are beautiful at this time of year. Perfect for cross-country skiing, even if we have to break trail ourselves. It's a perfect place for me to …"

I put down the hoof that, ostensibly, I had been examining. My hand covered my brother's as it lay on the stallion's back. Meeting his eye, I nodded. "Yes, you are right. They are beautiful. Peaceful in their pristine majesty. A good choice, brother."

I informed our sire the following morning that I would be assessing Charles' winter survival skills. I realised from my sire's flinched that my eyes had changed in that manner that others found disconcerting.

"Assessing his winter skills? You know that he is scheduled for the ring in a week's time?" My sire growled, his fists clenched on the surface of the desk in his office.

"We will be gone two days. It will take that long to reach a suitable point in the Laurentian Mountains. Away from the beaten track is best for … certain tasks." I stated. There was no emotion in my tone. My sire was no stupid.

"Indeed." My sire's lips curled upwards. "Two days?" He nodded. "Very well. I am sure you will demonstrate your usual efficiency in carrying out your brother's assessment."

That was all it took. I packed equipment for myself, and Charles packed his own, as befitted our purported purpose of skiing cross-country. My brother seemed at peace with his choice, and that was what I had told myself. It was his choice.

My sire had left orders. On my return, alone, I was ushered into his office. It had been the office of the Alpha before him, but the ambience was different now. Laurent stood in his usual place, behind our sire's chair, ever eager to implement orders as Beta of the Gosselin Pack.

"Well?" My sire's voice was a low growl.

"I regret to inform you that Charles failed his winter survival training." My response suggested there was more. But, in a blatant disregard of my sire's position as Alpha, I turned on my heel to leave the room. I heard Laurent move, but before his hand could land on my shoulder, I suggested that he think twice. "Accidents happen, brother." The sneer in my voice was clear. "It would be a shame if the Pack needed a new Beta."

Neither of them moved. I had insulted the Alpha, and made a veiled threat to the Beta. Under ordinary circumstances, I had just signed my own death warrant. It revealed much that neither spoke as I left the room to return to my own quarters.

Sixteen years old and my reputation was set. The Psycho Gosselin was a force to be feared.

CHAPTER 14 – MAKING PLANS

The brooding look across his sire's features did not bode well, not for the focus of that look, I remember thinking. I was right. I may have been just shy of eighteen, but in the twelve years I had lived in my sire's home, or rather in home of my step-dam, Janice, I had learned much. My sire saw us all as commodities, to be used or discarded as seemed appropriate. If we did not serve to increase the Pack's wealth, then we were irrelevant.

Unfortunately for Alix, she was not in that category. Home for the holiday season, her first since she started to attend Miss Porter's, she was showing signs of the beauty she would be in time.

"I have received offers for her already." My sire grunted. "Her net worth is far more than I anticipated." He glanced at me. "Inspired suggestion that I permit her to live when she was born, boy." The look in my sire's eyes became even more covetous, as he saw Alix's monetary worth only.

I had a fairly good idea of what sort of male my sire would deem a suitable mate for Alix. Her life would be hell, plain and simple, possibly even worse that her dam, Janice, because the first mating could take place as soon as her seasonal cycle was confirmed, which could be any time now. Our sire would not give a shit that Alix might not be physically capable of bearing young.

Damn, but the whole intention of sending her to Miss Porter's was that she mixed with a group of young ladies from influential backgrounds: captains of industry, politicians, families with old money, just like the public face of the Gosselin family. That way, her disappearance into a mating would be noticed, and questions raised. But this early into her schooling at Miss Porter's, the excuse of boarding school not suiting Alix would be acceptable.

This could not be allowed to happen. That much I knew. I was nearly of an age myself when I might conceivably be able to leave the compound, particularly after I had received a confidential letter from a firm of lawyers, informing me that on reaching eighteen, I would inherit a significant amount from my late dam. The word significant did not even come close to the actual figure cited. It was enough that I could establish my own home in New York, and work from offices there, rather than under the eye of my sire. However, I could not leave if there was a risk that Alix would be mated off and forced to bear pups at the risk to her own life.

The problem was that the person with whom I needed to discuss plans had to be careful herself. Sending a text message to her, telling her that they needed to talk was the only way. Burn phone to burn phone, and Goddess grant that no one found out.

Janice had just left the room raising her shaking hand to the help block the pain in her left eye where she had been struck, in public, when she heard the small soft beep which alerted her to the fact she had a text message waiting. Janice had looked over her shoulder, her posture slightly hunched over, checking that her mate had not decided to follow her. I knew that when she saw the message was from me, she would respond, but only when it was safe to do so. The norm after such an incident was that she would retire to her rooms, and endeavour to cover the evidence of her mate's handiwork with the supply of concealing cosmetics which she kept to hand. She would also know that it had to be important for me to want to talk with her; it must have something to do with her daughter, Alix.

The vibration of my phone told me that Janice had replied to my message on the need to meet. Where could they meet, where there was no chance of being overheard by someone with more to gain by reporting their actions back to my sire? Damn, that eliminated most of the compound.

Standing abruptly, I caught my sire's attention. "As we have guests coming tomorrow, I need to give the Pup another lessoning, sir, so that he recalls how he should comport himself in company." My statement was in the cold tone that was the norm for the Psycho Gosselin, the name which I knew others used for me, ever since Charles' mysterious death in the mountains. The 'Pup' was his youngest sibling, Adhémar, the legitimate heir to the Gosselin Alpha title through being Janice's only male offspring. The true heir and therefore, a threat to my other brother, my sire's 'Mini-Me', Laurent.

"Indeed. The pack wishing to mate their eldest female, Christelle, to Laurent ..." He patted his heir apparent's shoulder, "... will be coming tomorrow. Ensure that the Pup knows his place and causes no trouble. Chain him in his room if you must, but there must be no doubt in the minds of the Bouchard pack that Laurent is not the heir."

Hiding his own anger at the casual way that his sire had backhanded Janice, without a care that others saw, I realised that I had the perfect solution which would allow him to converse with Janice. "Perhaps the Pup's dam should watch whilst I administer the lessoning, sir? It would remind her that she must hold her tongue with our visitors?" My sire smiled.

"An excellent idea, boy. Let me know if she fails to understand the message." His clear glee that he might be able to hurt her further was sickening. However, it would work, as a plan. Janice and I might converse, might design a plan to protect Alix without anyone interrupting us. I might have to ensure that Adhémar was unconscious, but it would mean that we might talk in the small room that was the Pup's personal space.

Janice had already told him, in a rare show of spirit, that she hoped no one found out she was looking for a way to prevent Alix's early mating from happening. If they did the slight beating she just received would be no more than a playful slap. If she was lucky, Pierre would let her die. If she was lucky. The looks of pity and scorn she was getting from some the pack were an insult, but she knew she had to find way to protect her children first then she would work on herself.

I couldn't help but see the attempt to conceal the latest bruises on her face, and I wanted to snarl. Rather than targeting my youngest sibling, I wanted the object of my anger to be my sire and Laurent. But my mystery mentor, the male who had contacted me around the same time as the lawyers had hinted that their time would come and it would not be at my hands.

As we came around the corner, and a quick inhalation assured me that there was no one around, I touched a gentle finger to the growing bruise on Janice's face. I had done this before, with both Janice, Adhémar and others. How it helped, I didn't know, but the bruises would not be as painful, or the broken bone would heal faster. It was small recompense for what my sire inflicted on them.

As we approached Adhémar's room, I gave Janice an ironic bow. "The Alpha has suggested that I have a word with you and your pup, prior to the arrival of the Bouchard pack tomorrow." With my face set to the cold lines of the Psycho Gosselin, I opened the door to Adhémar's small room, and gestured for Janice to enter.

Adhémar had been curious to see what was going on so he had sneaked to the top of the stairs, staring at all the males that packed the room. He saw that Alix and I had caught him staring so he took off running toward his room, the only place he was truly allowed to be. He had just settled down on his bed when he would have heard my voice, to him the voice of the one bastard that sent cold shivers down his spine. If I was here that only meant one thing: a beating.

I could not let my true thoughts show on my face, regardless of how I felt at the sight of my youngest sibling, a 'pup' of nine years, huddled against the wall on his bed, his legs drawn up into a seated foetal position, his arms wrapped around his knees, everything about his posture screaming that he knew that he was about to suffer a beating from his tormentor.

I saw Adhémar's eyes widen at the sight of his dam behind me, and knew that the pup's mind would be running riot of why his dam was here. Was this some new form of torture for his dam, that she must witness him being 'educated' by me?

"Your Alpha has requested that I ... instruct you on correct behaviour to your betters, particularly when the Bouchard Pack visits tomorrow, to discuss Laurent's mating." I could not allow my lip to curl at the thought that I would have to 'squire' the younger Bouchard female, Fabienne, given that I was officially Laurent's second. "You had best make this easy, pup. I have no wish to waste my time with something as trivial as you. Kneel over the end of the bed ..." I pulled the supple leather belt from my trousers, as if I intended to use it on the younger male. "Bare yourself so that you may take your punishment as a Gosselin." I forced myself to keep my voice cold, the tone clipped and harsh. "Move, pup. I have no wish to miss my dinner because of you. Don't worry, this won't show on your pretty little face. Our guests will be quite taken with your meek and well-mannered behaviour tomorrow, I am sure."

I watched as the younger male did as he was ordered, even as I could hear Janice's whimper of pain for her son. Just then, the door opened, and I scented my sister, Alix. Merde! This was just what I didn't need.

"Go back downstairs, sister." I sneered. "This does not concern you."

I knew that Janice's heart would be thumping hard in her chest. She hated to see this battle of wills between her children, knowing that I hated this as much as she did. She was wringing her hands nervously, no doubt aware of how many times Pierre had ordered me to punish Adhémar this way. Her hand went to her own face which had only moments ago been throbbing with pain, from the shattered bones that were now healing in her cheek.

"Adhémar, please son, just do as he says you know what will happen if you resist". She watched mournfully my brother unfolded himself, scooting to the end of the bed and lowering his trousers, presenting his butt for his brother to lash. Janice wanted to desperately stay my hand but she knew if she did, chances were that I would be forced to do more than what I had planned. If I was forced to beat Adhémar in public, as had happened before, protecting him from major injury was nigh on impossible. This was only to be for show, the real reason for this was so that we could work out how to protect Alix from becoming a pawn in my sire's game of power. Janice turned suddenly when she felt her daughter's presence behind her and cringed visibly when she saw the hatred that had shown in her daughter's eyes, when she looked at me brandishing the thin belt as I lifted it in preparation to strike the trembling Adhémar.

I sneered at Alix as she looked as if she would try to wrestle the belt from me. "Have you not suitors to impress, you silly little bitch." Deliberately, I used a harsh tone and insulting words. "Several offers have been made for you already." I looked her up and down, still sneering. "You are not bad for breeding stock. Sturdy, young enough to produce healthy pups and not lose blossom of youth too soon." I gave a bark of laughter. "After all, your mating will last as long as necessary. It won't be the first time a young male has met with an unfortunate accident, and you are young enough that the 'widow' can be a coveted spouse in another pack." I smiled, a cold smile, the Psycho Gosselin smile. Let her think that our sire would continue to 'sell' her as a mate as often as necessary for him to continue to accrue wealth and influence. "How surprising. Who would have guessed that a mere female could be so useful? Breeding stock and a tool to be used for political gain." Deliberately I turned my back on her, running the supple leather of my belt through my hands, as if I could not wait to apply it to Adhémar's skin.

With her mother standing there, watching me about to punish Adhémar for who knew what, an involuntary growl escaped Alix as she glanced at her dam with all the loathing she could muster. To her, it must seem that her dam's lack of maternal instincts had more than earned her daughter's disgust. If there was ever a reason for Alix to question the sanctity of mating it was at this very moment. Alix could never be cowed down to the point of allowing her own children suffer the way her dam clearly allowed. She moved closer, her hand stretching out to take the belt away from me. Alix had no problems taking a beating for her brother, she stopped at my words. She stood there listening to the truths I uttered about her current situation. Even at a relatively young age, Alix was very much aware of her sire's plans for her, hearing it from her brother's own mouth was a stab on her pride, as I intended, and a reminder that her life was not her own, not yet.

Defeated, she turned around giving one last glare at her mother. She would have taken but a couple of steps towards the stairs when she would have heard the belt hit flesh. I could imagine her, clutching her fists on her dress with such force it would leave crease marks. There was no point in returning now, the damage was done. One day, one day, to her mind, I would receive my just rewards. One day she would not need to come and stay over the holidays. Even so young, what Alix was learning was that she needed to be strong.

I could almost feel the pain from Janice when she heard the belt meet the skin of her son's bare backside, the lash mark red and raised, the soft whine from Adhémar at the strike. I knew that she worried if he would ever understand that they had just been trying to protect him and his sister. She worried he would come to hate her as the weak female she had found herself becoming. Janice gasped when Adhémar slumped against the bed in a deep sleep. She looked at me. "Will he be alright?"

As the door slammed shut, I had struck my younger brother once, the belt leaving a noticeable welt across the younger male's skin. Leaning forward as if to admire my handiwork, I touched two fingers to the side of Adhémar's neck, watching as my brother dropped forward, unconscious. I listened for a moment, hearing the even breaths that denoted that my brother was unconscious but breathing unimpaired. "Yes, he will bear the mark of my belt, which will suffice for our Alpha." My lip curled at using that title for my sire. "But, he will attribute his lack of pain to the fact that he has become accustomed to these ... lessons."

I looked at the door for a moment, listening, taking a deep breath to ensure that Alix had not lingered on the other side of the door. "We must be quick, before anyone else disturbs us. We must come up with a way that Alix will be safe. As it stands, she could be brought home and mated, and the school given the excuse that she was homesick. It happens." I shook his head.

"We must find a way to prevent that happening. Money is seen as a sign of importance. I will foster rumours that Alix is heiress to an unspecified but significant inheritance. Does she still have that fascination with the law and police work?" Pierre Gosselin had been disgusted with Alix's interest. Good enough reason to encourage her.

"If I set up a college scholarship fund for her, and convince my sire that this money was given by a mystery benefactor, then I can suggest it is a mark of his influence that someone has made this offer for his daughter." I gave another harsh bark of laughter. "I will make it sound plausible, perhaps mentioning the funds came from an investor in another of our projects? That way, he won't wish to antagonise an investor. It will give us something of a breathing space."

"Janice." I touched his step-dam's arm, the look on her face saying only too clearly how she felt in the face of the damning look, the disgust on Alix's face. "She has to believe the fiction." My voice was quiet. "If she thinks that for one moment this is an elaborate ruse, we are all dead meat. As it stands, Pierre Gosselin has too many followers. I can't kill them all, not together."

I glanced back at the still unconscious Adhémar. "He also must believe the fiction. I don't care if they both hate me. If it means we stop Pierre, the price will be worth it." For a moment, I wondered if I had said that for Janice's benefit or for my own.

"You have already been on the receiving end of his temper tonight. He won't do anything with the guests around, so you will be safe downstairs." My smile was grim. "You know the usual: look cowed, keep your eyes down." I had sighed. "You shouldn't have to know all this, may that bastard rot in the fires of the underworld. If only the Cwn Annwn were not a myth." I wished, referring to the legendary servants of the Goddess.

"I will set up the scholarship fund and the e-mail trail that demonstrates it came from an anonymous backer of one of the other 'projects'. There will be time to discuss it tomorrow, before the Bouchard pack arrive."

CHAPTER 14 – A NEAR MISS

The mating of my elder brother Laurent had been deemed to be a time of celebration for the Gosselin Pack, since my sire had decided that it was the next best thing to a human royal wedding. Who was the lucky recipient of this favour? It was the eldest female offspring of the Alpha of the Bouchard pack, a smaller pack than our own but with connections and the mating was to ensure that those connections were open to the use of the Gosselin Alpha. Of course, in time, Laurent would be the Gosselin Alpha and I would be his "faithful" Gosselin Beta. The female in question was Christelle. She was the same age as Laurent and she also had a younger sister, Fabienne. The difference between the two sisters could not have been more different. Both cultivated the appearance of society females, whose main interest was parties and events at which they might be photographed. That such events were both shifter society and human society was not held against them, interestingly enough, particularly given my sire's ambivalence towards humans. As I said they cultivated the appearance of being, to be blunt, airheads. The younger female, Fabienne, was anything but an airhead.

To coin a human phrase, it takes one to know one. I do not believe I am being conceited but I knew that I had an above-average ability in terms of computers and in terms of using the information that I could gather both from legitimate and, shall we say, less salubrious sources. When I met Fabienne, I am not sure whether it was the look in her eye, the hint of a smirk, the slightly stronger grip when she took my hand? What I did know was that as much as I cultivated the impression of being the Psycho Gosselin, Fabienne cultivated the impression of being as unintelligent as her sister. The impression that I had of the younger Bouchard female was that she was playing a similar game to my own. I don't mean to say that she was a psychopath in hiding or that she was a candidate for the Nobel Peace Prize. But, undoubtedly, she was hiding something. That in itself made me reluctant to associate with her.

However that feeling that she was hiding something was not the reason why I referred to my encounter with her as a near miss. I knew that my sire planned that I would be Laurent's second-in-command when Laurent became the Alpha of the Gosselin Pack. So what would be more convenient than for the Beta in Waiting of the Gosselin Pack to be mated to the sister of the future Alpha's mate? Again I shall use a human phrase. Hell, no! What else can I say, in the face of my sire's brilliant idea? The only thing that saved me was that Christelle's sister had an almost identical look of dismay on her face to my own when the suggestion was put forward. There had been laughter, as my sire and the Bouchard Alpha had joked that perhaps this second mating was not as popular with the potential participants as with their sires.

The frustrating thing for me was that at the time instincts were screaming that there was something I was missing about the impression that I had on the younger Bouchard female. The problem was I could not figure out what it was I was missing and to say that I was uncomfortable with the proposed mating between us would have been insufficient for my sire to agree that the proposal should be put to one side. Instead I had to find another way to convince him that his brilliant plan was anything but brilliant. The solution turned out to be quite simple. My sire was inordinately proud of Laurent since my elder sibling was his choice to succeed to the title of Alpha in due course. Thus, in order to convince my sire that a double mating was a bad plan, all I had to do was remind him that a double mating would take away some of the glory of Laurent's own mating. Perish the thought that I might wish to even slightly upstage my elder sibling. This was Laurent's time to shine, I told my sire. Any plans for my own mating could wait. It had been far too close to call. Far too close.

The other thing that was frustrating for me was that when I tried to investigate this Bouchard female, the available information using all my usual sources, was sparse. That in itself raised flags for me. The sources of information that I would use contained both public and private information. Some of my sources were, as one might say, not quite legal, and there was the fact that, with my sire having several law enforcement professionals in his pocket, it was possible to access their sources as well. Of course, I would not necessarily help them that I was using their passwords to access those sources. To my mind, if they were that careless that a hacker could access their passwords and thus their so-called confidential databases, they only had themselves to blame.

When I think about it now, that lack of information seemed almost as if it was there to be found. If my sire had decided to put his plan of a double mating into action, then I may well have looked further. But at the time, once he had agreed that the important mating was my brother's, searching for information on Fabienne Bouchard did not become a priority. The question would be whether that decision would come back to haunt me.

In the meantime I had to put up with both Bouchard females, and if I had tried to avoid the younger female, I had even more cause to avoid the elder, Christelle, who was rapidly demonstrating that she was more than a suitable match for Laurent in terms of her scorn towards not just the pack that would be hers to "rule" when her mate became Alpha, but also towards Janice, as the mate of the existing Alpha. She was also dismissive of both Alix and Adhémar. The latter was hardly surprising since my youngest sibling was not expected to amount to anything. So to a mind as shallow as Christelle's, what point was there in cultivating him.

Even if it was decided that Fabienne and I would not be celebrating a double Mating with Laurent, I was still expected to escort her to dinner. That necessitated some conversation, but when my gut instinct was telling me that she was concealing something about herself, that was going to be interesting. I opted for a supposedly safe subject, namely college education, and wasn't that a surprise.

She had frowned before admitting, "I am a Cal-Tech graduate." She had almost snapped at me. Of course, that was the information I had on her from my initial research.

"MIT, myself." I was equally brusque. This wasn't a good topic. Inter-college rivalry should never be underestimated, particularly with tech graduates. "So, not the best conversational topic, but our respective sires are going to expect to see us being pleasant to each other."

"Fine. Stock market fluctuations." She suggested as a topic for conversation. "I know you take care of the financials for the Gosselin Pack. I do the same for the Bouchard Pack."

I gave a bark of laughter. "You expect me to divulge financials? Girl, you must be tripping." My voice dripped sarcasm. "The weather will become boring. How about outdoor activities? As I recall, your Facebook profile had pictures of you and Christelle going skiing."

Fabienne gave a half smile. "I think we might manage about half an hour's conversation on that one."

It wasn't my first choice of topic. I was still responsible for the winter survival training within the Pack, and since Charles' suicide, much to my sire's dismay, more were passing first time. I was determined that it should not be used as a convenient means of disposing of those who crossed Pierre Gosselin.

Now, I know the reason for that frisson of distaste that it crossed my features when my sire had made his brilliant suggestion. I would not have wanted to be mated to another female, because ultimately I would find my predestined mate in Daniela.

CHAPTER 15 – AN INHERITANCE AND A MENTOR

Until such time as I moved away from the Gosselin compound, my mentor, for lack of a better description, had contacted me via e-mails or text messages. It was only when I had my own apartment, the same one I retained in New York now, that I was to meet him for the first time. Was that a surprise?

I knew he was male and I had a contact number, but that was all. Given his role in my life, and given that he said he was a contemporary of my late dam, I had expected someone a tad older, but that was part of it, as I was to discover. Categorically, I can say that I did not expect the male in their late 20s or early 30s that he appeared to be. He was suited when he showed up at my apartment, but it was also apparent that this was not his normal mode of dress, as evidenced by the way he yanked the tie away, dropping it and the jacket across the back of a dining chair, before throwing himself into one of the armchairs.

I had raised a brow. "Make yourself at home, why don't you?" My comment held more than a tad of sarcasm. If it wasn't for the fact that I had been in correspondence, of sorts, with this individual for over a year, my reaction might have been different. This place was my sanctuary, where I did not have to play the part of Casimir Gosselin, the second son and 'brains' behind the Gosselin financial empire. So, I threw myself in the opposite armchair, having first placed my cut-crystal tumbler of Scottish single malt on the side table. "At least we have now met." I took a sip of the whisky. "Are you going to give me a name, finally?"

"Zarek." The male's voice had a hint of a European accent, slightly guttural, so I was guessing that he was Eastern

European. "Zarek Svitovidson." The male smiled, and it was the smile of a predator. "As for who I am, that's easy. I am your uncle. Your dam's brother, to be precise, before you think me related to that piece of shit that sired you."

Years of schooling my features to indifference enabled me to hide my reaction to his introduction. "My uncle." I was thoughtful. "You are my uncle." I knew it sounded a bit daft repeating what he had just said. "My question would have to be why you waited until now to introduce yourself? After all, I received your first communication over a year ago."

My uncle, Zarek, snorted with laughter. "Knowing your father, you have to ask that question?" This was the start of what I would come to see as the norm for Zarek. Rarely would he give me a straight answer. He had his reasons, which I would come to appreciate, but then? No, it was just ever so slightly irritating that I had to feel as if I needed to interrogate him to find an answer.

He did share one useful piece of information and that was clarifying that he was, in fact, my dam's half-brother. They shared a sire. He also explained that my dam was of Native Canadian stock. "Stock being the operative word. When the lawyers contacted me, it was a bit surprising. Do you realise what my sire would have done to me if he knew that I concealed that communication, both its nature and its implications?" After all, with my sire's drive for power and wealth, learning that his second son had just inherited funds which made the Gosselin empire look moderate? It would be safe to say that he would have been livid.

"Trust me." My newly discovered uncle had laughed. "Your dam and I had no intention of your sire ever finding out who she was. The important thing was, from our point of view anyway, was that you appreciated exactly the measure of your sire." Zarek's lip had curled at the mention of Pierre Gosselin. It was safe to say that my uncle did not have a very high opinion of my sire, but then, as he had pointed out, living under my sire's rule as long as I had I had a very low opinion of him as well.

"Clearly building that sort of level of financial security must serve a purpose?" I asked my uncle

"Well, duh! Of course it served a purpose." Clearly Zarek was back to his usual, as I was to discover, taciturn self.

"Okay, so quite clearly I have to guess what this purpose might be?" I took a sip of my single malt Scotch savouring the taste. "How about I tell you what I would like to do."

My uncle and I had passed the evening much in the same way. I had tried to prise information from him and he had continued to play his game of forcing me to think or to guess, however you want to put it. That said, it was safe to say that by the end of the evening, I did not feel so soiled by some of the things I had been ordered to do by my sire.

There was one other aspect which my uncle was to offer advice. In establishing some of the less salubrious business ideas of my sire, I had become more than familiar with the Dark Net. After all, that was where he found customers for his 'product', be that product guns, drugs or other 'commodities'. Regarding the latter, all I could do at that stage was to build a backdoor into the system which logged sources and destinations. I kept meticulous records, in fact, not just of the commodities in which my sire chose to deal, but also in terms of communications with those who eased the path for our business affairs. In time, I promised myself, in time. I know that Zarek was aware of how I felt, because he was there when the feeling of being soiled became almost unbearable. He would whisk me away to somewhere else, using the opportunity, he said, to teach me how to travel on my own. Travel, flash, teleport. However you wish to describe it, it was a skill which came as a surprise, but a welcome one. Whilst skiing through untouched black run country might not allow me to forget, at least the solitude enabled me to gather my own internal resources.

All I could promise myself was, "One day."

Exploration of the Dark Net was, strangely, something which Zarek encouraged. He hadn't said much beyond that. Through that vast resource of information, I encountered a couple of, shall we call them kindred spirits. We would know each other only by our handles: BadWolf76, BowmanWolf and RedDragon01. I used to smile at the latter. The '01' designation was there in the face of anyone else who thought to adopt a similar handle. It screamed, "Go away, little creature. I am the first and the original." Now, of course, I know that RedDragon01 had good reason to use the name, but then, I thought it merely some form of conceit and self-aggrandisement. How wrong would I prove to be?

CHAPTER 16 – NEW PROJECTS (EVENTS IN ALPHA)

The way that my sire chose to exploit the human world around us started in a relatively small scale manner. Hurricane Katrina was a prime example. His business interests at the time were primarily in the casino boats anchored just off the Biloxi coast and some of the places operating in the City of New Orleans itself. There were many things which contributed to the destruction, loss of life and of livelihoods. I won't rehash them here. There was one detail, and it very nearly exposed some of my other activities to my sire.

After the hurricane came the rebuilding. Part and parcel of that were some fairly large contracts, and certainly, anyone who had a significant interest in construction was going to be competing on those contracts. Corruption is something that most will assume occurs in other countries, never on the blessed soil of America. It would be delightful if their faith in their fellow man could be validated, and yes, organisations like Habitat 4 Humanity and similar did excellent work. But there was always opportunities for those less altruistic.

My sire had barged into my assigned 'office' in the Gosselin Compound complex on hearing about the hurricane and the loss of the casino boats. It was also patently obvious that it would be a while before things were back to normal. He demanded to know what plans I had for making up the shortfall in the Gosselin Pack income stream. As it happened, I had open on one of the two screens on my desk a list of the contracts up for tender for the rebuilding. I had the information up because I was diverting some of my own funds to proven charitable organisations. Pierre Gosselin had pounced on the list.

"On how many have you put in bids, boy?" He demanded.

I may have reached adult years, but it was normal for him to use words like that in a pathetic attempt to stress that he was above you in the Pack hierarchy.

"I have half a dozen bids out, mostly on public buildings. They are the ones most likely to choose cost over any other considerations." I was watching them for that very purpose. A shortcut on the quality of the timber used or bring in materials from less than ethical sources, all these would enable the contractor to trim the bid to a level acceptable in a cost-conscious economy.

The fact that I was also using the process as a means of identifying individuals with less than sterling morals was neither here nor there. Public officials would suggest re-election campaign donations. Donations or bribes? Ask yourself that question. Strange how many of them were in a position to influence the awarding of those contracts. Nothing blatant, mind you. Perish the thought that I might be accusing the officials of that City of profiting from human misery. I had to cover my tracks in terms of my own donations, so I took steps to ensure that we did have one contract awarded to us. It also enabled me to verify my concerns over the flexible morals involved in the process. All this was added to my files. "Later." I would promise myself.

There's a big difference between the occasional crooked building contract or involvement in legal gambling such as operated on the shoreline of Biloxi, and the next stage of my sire's idea of profitable businesses. It had been one of Janice's concerns, that my sire would move the Pack's business emphasis away from the legal interests of her sire's day, to the purely for profit and legality be damned that Pierre preferred. I had assured her that I would endeavour to maintain as much of those industries as I could, which was one of the reasons why I had to move away from the Gosselin compound, visiting only when I had no choice, when I had to be seen in order to ensure that no one supplanted me as the apparent Beta Designate.

When my sire first outlined his plan, which he referred to as an extension to farming, I had to hide the nausea that his suggestion induced. The casual way in which he thought he might use humans both male and female as a means of making money beggared belief. His avowal that they were less than us, less than a wolf shifters, was deliberate. It was intended to set the impression in pack members minds that it was no different to the way humans would farm cattle or any other livestock. He wanted the pack to believe that they were superior and that this was only there "right".

But this went beyond deliberately cultivating addicts need for narcotics. This went far beyond that. As he outlined his plan the sinking feeling I had was that I had little choice but to be involved, because it was the only way that I would have information on everything: the set-up, the customers, the officials whom he would need to bribe so that his endeavours were not investigated. All those little details.

The fact that my sire could purchase the loyalty of human officials, those same human officials who were trusted to be honest in their public offices, demonstrated to me that humans shared some aspects in common with wolf shifters, even if my sire wanted everyone to see them as an inferior species. Thus, we come onto the subject of Detective Johnson of the Vice Squad. I'm fairly certain that humans meant that to infer he fought against vice rather than attempted to see where he might assist its existence.

One thing I did know was that when the time came, I would take great pleasure in ensuring that Detective Johnson learnt the price for his attitude to those whom he should have been protecting. That was something that seemed to be important to me. I was realising that, the longer I was away from the Gosselin compound. I didn't view humans as deficient, in the way that my sire did. At the same time, I knew that there were things that I could do which they could not. It was no different to, say, a talented artist compared to a marksman. Just a case of different abilities and skill sets.

Individuals like Detective Johnson were more interested in self-aggrandisement, rather than protecting those who were weaker. How he liked to strut his stuff in front of the cameras, taking pleasure in being the 'Golden Boy', who was breaking up the drug rings which had plagued the state for so long. That those rings were being replaced by agents of my sire, and that Johnson was taking significant kickbacks to ignore them was not an issue to the Vice Department human. Protect and uphold the law? Yeah, right.

But going back to those plans. He had identified two very profitable sources of income. Sex, the oldest trade in the world, and drugs. Within the former, there were those that had very specific tastes and more importantly from Pierre Gosselin's perspective, they had the money to ensure that their proclivities did not cause them trouble with the law or with anyone in authority. Add 'suppliers' such as my sire intended to become, and you had a 'secure' business. What did it matter that young human females disappeared periodically? What did it matter that intelligent young women, whose only 'crime' was to lack close family, ended their lives in pain and terror? Profit. My sire had slammed his fist on the desk. Profit was what mattered.

The problem was that my sire's attitude spawned other ideas which could be made to look acceptable because of the profit potential. As the Pack's financier, I knew about most of them, but there were some that slipped under my net, forcing me to play catch up.

"You can't catch them all." Zarek tried reasoning with me one evening at my New York apartment.

"If I don't, then who the hell can, or will even attempt to track the money trail?" I was pouring us both some coffee, because I knew that if I resorted to alcohol, I would drink myself into a frustrated stupor. "I know there is something going on. Funds have been diverted. That much I know. The coding used indicates a 'medical project' which is my sire's euphemism for a drug-related project. But it is not going to the usual dealing networks."

"You have tracked most of what your sire has set up." Zarek pointed out.

"Most is not all." I ran my hands through my hair impatiently, trying to gather my thoughts so I could explain to him why this was important. I hadn't missed the way that Zarek's eyes had narrowed which told me that he was … not testing me, but certainly challenging me.

"Look, I know I can't stop all the drug dealing in the continental USA. But, I have promised Janice that Adhémar will have a clean set of finances to inherit, when Pierre receives his just desserts. So far I have managed to keep track of everything that my sire is doing, but since I moved away from the compound, I have reason to believe that he has someone else dabbling in the accounts." I explained.

"Will they track your own finances?" Zarek asked.

"Not a chance." I said that without being immodest. Since I had found out the extent of my inheritance, I had taken pains to conceal it from my sire. "No, my issue is that if he does start using someone else, I lose my influence. I don't want to have to move back to the Gosselin compound if I can avoid it. I need the freedom of living away, just to maintain my damned sanity." My laugh lacked mirth. "Can you an imagine a shifter with OCD symptoms of hand-washing in view of scum with whom I would have to associate?"

"Your sire's time will come. I have said that before. I can say that it won't be at your hands, but you will have a role to play." Zarek gave that enigmatic smile that told me he was imparting something from his divination side.

"It can't come soon enough." I retorted. I flopped down into one of the armchairs. "I might as well enjoy this evening. I will have to return to the compound. My sire has a closed network up there, which he installed about six months ago. That's where I need to look. I might as well enjoy my freedom while it lasts."

CHAPTER 17 – ALIX MEETS HER MATE

The day that my sire found out that he and the rest of the pack were invited to meet a mystery pack in New York State, living out in the Catskills, will be a memory hard to forget. To put it bluntly, my sire had been incandescent with rage. He had tried to play what he thought to be Alix's game, from the time that she had finished at Miss Porter's School, and gone straight into summer school classes to gain additional college credit. She had learned well, and made a point of making friends on campus, both with fellow students and with her professors, so that if she were to 'go missing' on our sire's orders, it would be noticed. It would not be a good plan for a popular student of Criminal Justice, who made it clear that she intended to become a homicide detective with the State Police, to disappear. Questions would have been asked, as Alix knew only too well.

The upshot was this invitation to dinner from the Negrescu Pack based in the Catskills. This was where I started to play my own version of 'Cat and Mouse' with my sire. I knew that my sire would wish to ensure that he had a full dossier on this mystery pack. I wanted information for myself, but I had no intention of furnishing that information to my sire. That meant he would have to rely on Laurent's skills for gathering the information. My elder sibling had become sloppy and as a result, he tended to rely on information which I might provide. My sudden unavailability meant that, in the 48 hours he had available to him, Laurent had to provide our sire with something. Grainy photographs taken with a telephoto lens were not going to be sufficient, but I had to admire my sister's gall. She would have known that our sire would be watching, or rather sending others to watch. She knew that being seen climbing onto the back of a Harley Davidson bike outside of the Police HQ would be just about enough to rile our sire, and I have every reason to believe that she did so deliberately. Let us not forget that Alix was as much the daughter of Pierre Gosselin as the daughter of Janice Gosselin.

I knew that, in the role of second-in-command to Laurent, my sire would expect me to attend the dinner at Negrescu Hall. But if there was one thing that working with my uncle had taught me, it was the value of knowing your position. So, if I were to look at the situation in a more dispassionate manner, what would I see? From the photographs that had been taken of my sister's new interest, he gave every impression of being a biker, a Harley Davidson riding biker. Place that against the fact that my sire put great importance on the way that others perceived members of the Gosselin Pack and thus him, and you had an interesting situation brewing. A biker and a cop. Or, to put it another way an individual who gave every appearance of skirting the edges of the law, of being uneducated, uncouth, rough, no doubt with the manners of a pig; this individual had the temerity to think, to dare to think, that he might be suitable relationship material for the Gosselin princess, as my sister was known. Appearances were everything to my sire and this unknown male was everything which he held in derision.

So, to my mind, that meant that there must be a lot more to this liaison than was immediately apparent. Whilst my sire tasked others with investigating this male further, I started to make my own enquiries, starting with the name of Negrescu.

The curious thing came when I tried to find more information on this Negrescu Pack. Let me make it clear. I did not intend to furnish this information to my sire. I wanted it for myself. I wanted to be sure that everything that Janice and I had done would not go to waste because my sister had found her Mate.

Where else would I search but the Dark Web.

Interesting was an understatement. I would find some information and that, in a tantalising manner, it would disappear, not leaving a blank which would indicate deleted information, but seamlessly, as if the information had never existed. The best I could find was that Negrescu was a common Eastern European name. That gave me pause. A common Eastern European name. And I had an uncle of Eastern European origins. Don't you just love coincidences?

What might have started as a semi-idle search for information became much more at that point. I didn't like coincidences then and I still don't like them now. Negrescu was the Eastern European form of the surname 'Black'. If I could have groaned online, I would have done. Black? Could they have been any more vague? Did that make them black wolves, or white, because they might choose to take a name opposite to the truth? There were no packs listed on the usual shifter databases by either name, a detail which had me thumping my desk in frustration. It was almost as if they were ghosts, and that, on the Dark Net, was saying something. Then even that small amount of information would disappear. That same seamless 'now you see it, now you don't' type of disappearance. Was I being played? Well, if I was, then game on.

My wariness had proven wise. I had traced a family by the name of Negrescu to the Carpathians, had noted they bought a property in the Catskills in 1938 which had been renovated, no doubt at a significant cost. But it was the fact that the family came from Wales originally, that was the key piece of information. The final piece of the jigsaw had come from one of my hacker acquaintances. A polite suggestion to back off from my enquiries. My sire and Laurent had taken on more than just an 'unknown' shifter pack, and there was only one likely outcome.

Of course, would it cross my mind that I might share what I had found so far with my sire and with Laurent? No way in hell. My uncle had promised me that time would come when

Laurent and my sire would face justice. I found myself hoping fervently that that time had come.

The only way according to shifter law that my sire might hope to prevent my sister's mating was for her mate to prove unsuitable as, to put it bluntly, breeding stock. Before my sire had changed the way that Matings were conducted in the Gosselin Pack, pups would be told the stories of how somewhere out in the wider world, one individual existed, who would be the match of one soul. That was supposed to be the way that a mating might occur. But practicality had to play a role, even before my sire had concocted his idea of these virtually dynastic Matings. So it was suggested that the best way forward would be for a male to succeed at a challenge set by the female's pack. Before there is any suggestion that this did not allow for same-sex pairings, I would ask you to remember that a mating was generally seen as a means for producing young. Same-sex pairings serve an undoubted and very important use in a pack because if parents might be killed either through accident or deliberate intent, it would fall on such same-sex pairings to raise the orphaned pups. But for the purpose of mating, the challenge system existed to prove that a male and female pairing was a good choice for breeding purposes. The male had to prove that his genes deserved to be carried forward into the next generation.

That is all very well and good, but even this simple idea was corrupted by Pierre Gosselin. To his mind if a male seeking to mate into the Gosselin Pack could not survive a challenge to the death, then he was unsuitable. Given that, until Alex was born, my father would see Gosselin females as breeding stock only, it was highly unusual for him to allow a female to mate outside of the pack. Males might petition to enter the Gosselin Pack, but they would have to survive a fight against one of my sire's enforcers. If they didn't, then they were not strong enough for the Gosselin Pack. Of course if the enforcer was killed, then clearly his genes did not deserve to be carried forward.

The members of the shifter Council valued the level of
influence that my sire held over such a large territory. Maybe
valued is the wrong word to use; they were certainly wary of
his level of influence. As a result whilst they may not agree
with the way that challenges were run as far as our pack was
concerned, not once did they intervene. Whatever personal
opinions they might have held, none wished to cross my sire.
Pierre Gosselin, regardless of how he had twisted a perfectly
rational challenge ideal, was left to do as he wished. Money
and influence had bought him immunity. That is how it
appeared to everybody.

I suspect this was why, when the challenges were proposed to
Alex's future mate, no one had expected his pack to respond
in the way that they did. In retrospect, the clues were probably
there, that Bran was anything but a normal Wolf. But my
sire's arrogance meant that he failed to appreciate the
situation until it was too late. By then, the shifter Council had
found their teeth. With the backing of the Cŵn Annwn, my
sire's reign of terror over the Gosselin Pack and the potential
for Laurent to have followed suit was over.

A new Alpha would rule the Gosselin Pack and it was not
going to be me.

CHAPTER 18 – DELTA

As the Lear jet taxied to a stop in front of the Gosselin private hanger at the Buffalo-Lancaster Airfield, I noticed that one of my sire's bodyguards was waiting by the hanger doors. Even from a distance, the male's agitation was plain, in the way that he stood, in the way that his eyes scanned around constantly. Something had happened whilst I had been sorting out the little problem which had occurred in the UK, and it did not look like good news.

As I came down the steps of the plane, I recognised the guard as one whom had been loyal to my sire. My sire had not even realised that I had my own males within the Pack, who answered to me, who understood my vision for the Pack's future. But as this one was of my sire's lackeys, my first concern was that perhaps something had gone wrong with the plans which had been laid so many years ago.

Calmly, I approached the bodyguard, my brow raised in question. To my surprise, the male dropped to one knee on the tarmac. What the fuck?

"Casimir Gosselin, I swear my allegiance to you as the true Alpha of the Gosselin Pack." Now that might not be considered the most encouraging thing to hear.

"You are either going to make me very happy with you, or somewhat irritated. Which one is it." In view of this individual's allegiance, the persona of the Psycho Gosselin was need, my voice was quiet, almost purring. "Which one is it? Is my sire dead?" Without raising his eyes, the bodyguard nodded. "And Laurent?" Again, he nodded.

I studied the guard's demeanour. "But something did not go according to plan?" The bodyguard cringed before he swallowed. Only then did he answer.

"Sire, the Negrescu Pack. They are ALL Cŵn Annwn, not just the Alpha, Gavril Negrescu. The whole Pack." He stammered. "Your sire and Laurent were executed." He hesitated.

"And …?" My voice was no longer purring. The Psycho Gosselin might be a tad irritated by this turn of events.

"Your brother, Adhémar Gosselin, has assumed the role of Alpha, with the endorsement of the Shifter Council. The whole Pack is now his." The bodyguard's voice was almost a whisper.

"Not the whole Pack or you would not be here." I murmured. Perhaps I had not have considered that my youngest brother was ready to pull this off, but as I had pointed out to Zarek only recently, of greater concern were those interests which my sire had kept hidden. There were some things which were mine to handle.

"Who else has remained loyal?" I asked. The bodyguard mumbled some names. Six others. It would be as I had expected. "Tell them we are relocating to the alternative site." When the bodyguard hesitated, I shoved him with my boot. "Well? For what are you waiting?"

"What about the Negrescu Pack?" He asked.

"We need only ensure that they don't come near enough to us to judge or whatever it is that they do." I appeared to dismiss the Cŵn Annwn as an issue. "Now get your posterior in gear." Speed was of the essence, but I had been planning my contingency plan for years. I might have to wait some, but I would have the results that I wished to have.

I smiled

My sire was no longer my concern. The Cŵn Annwn had seen to that, quite impressively, I was told. Adhémar was now the Alpha of the Gosselin Pack, as he should be. But it did not put me in the clear. I had my sire's former loyalists flocking to my proverbial banner. I also had my own pack, but more of that later

I had two key matters I had to address. I had to shut down the remains of my sire's business enterprises. That was my priority. Moreover, I had to do so in a manner which slotted in with the plans of the Cŵn Annwn. Equally important was shutting down the humans in my sire's employ. I have mentioned the Vice Detective, but I had also identified an FBI Agent. They had the potential to harm the shifter world and specifically, the Gosselin Pack. After all my efforts to hand my brother a cleansed pack, I was not permitting a couple of crooked humans to wreck it.

The other matter was more complex, and was the reason why the FBI Agent had come to my notice. Lamashtu wanted her claws in Fane … again. My uncle and mentor had stepped in again. Things must come to pass, blah, blah. I really disliked these moments. Imagine, if you would , trying to work your way through a maze, in the dark, with the sort of tiny torch found in a Christmas cracker as your only light source. That's how it felt when Zarek used those words. I knew that there was every possibility that whatever 'must come to pass' would involve a risk to life, but whatever! My life had been lived on the edge constantly. Why should this be any different.

First things first, I had to shut down the kidnap ring. There was much more to that ring than the kidnap of young women. As I had mentioned, my father had the idea of 'farming'. He had a loyal customer base, and he wanted to maintain them as a source of income. He was selling them educated young women as sex toys, and when they died, he sold them another human. As might be implied in the use of the word 'toys', the buyers were not looking for a girl whom they would honour and keep in comfort, hence my sire referring to it as 'farming'.

The human authorities were involved, the Police Detective who partnered my sister, Alix, and the Vice Detective Johnson, whose job should have been eradicating the kidnapping scum, not taking a generous retainer to ignore what was happening in front of him. I knew from Zarek that the Cŵn Annwn planned to send one of their own, the mate of one of their Betas, under cover. This would enable her Mate and her Alpha to track her to the location where the other girls were being held. First things first: stop the shipment of any other girls, so that they might be rescued.

CHAPTER 19
FORMATION OF A PACK:
MARCUS

All Packs start from something, and my own was no different.
No, I don't mean the Pack comprised of those of my late
sire's lieutenants, who viewed me as his 'true' heir. They
were scum with whom I had to associate if I was to ensure
that my sire's legacy was absolutely nothing. I knew that I had
not known everything that my sire had done. Pierre Gosselin
was many things and stupid was not one of them. But, as I had
pointed out to Zarek, working alone was not always the best
way forward. I was not working alone by then, but it had been
a slow process. Above all, I had to ensure that there was no
way that what I viewed as my true Pack could be discovered
by my enemies. It was for a very simple reason. The true Pack
of the Psycho Gosselin, contrary to his public image of hating
humans, included both wolf shifters and humans in its
numbers. We came up with the name Hellfire Pack, because
over a slightly drunken evening, we had come to the
conclusion that it was where we would be headed if we were
ever discovered.

I needed individuals with specific skill sets for my Pack.
Based on what I was doing, tech skills were the first thing I
needed. Of course, the type of tech skills I required are
perhaps not to be found in the most law-abiding of citizens,
but on occasion, a close match might exist. The first
individual whom I approached I found after a discussion with
some military contractors who were involved in, supposedly,
the destruction of decommissioned weapons from the Middle
East. Supposedly. The good old US of A, courtesy of the
Second Amendment, will always have a market for weapons
of specific types. Remove the serial numbers, and decent
prices might also be charged by those who do not wish to

advertise themselves to law enforcement agencies. Needless to say, it was an area of business in which my sire would have a stake. Considering it meant doing business with those who would break the law in their own country, it stood to reason that I might be cautious when … socialising with them.

Back to my search for an individual with tech skills. I knew that the sort of individual I needed was likely to have a military background. Specialism in tech, but holding other skills also. Let's be blunt. I needed ex-Special Forces personnel.

It transpired that the 'best' person had been killed recently in a skirmish in the Middle East. A whole team of SEALS had been dropped into what appeared to be an ambush. Bad intel, my contact had shaken his head, but there had been something in his eyes which implied that there was much more to the story than an operation gone wrong. Next port of call had been my old friends in the Dark Web, Bowman and Dragon. That was where it became interesting. Those of us involved in the world of shadows still have something of a signature. To a certain extent, we want our work to be known almost as much as we want it to be untraceable. For those in the know, there was generally a way of discovering where information or an individual might be found.

Marcus Aurelius Jones was the individual's name. Leader of the team of SEALS, it was believed he had died in the deserts of the Middle East. Yet, if you knew where to look, there was evidence that he was certainly alive. It was just a matter of teasing him out of hiding.

The structure which I had in mind was to pair suitably skilled humans with a wolf-shifter partner. The skill sets would be matched but it would mean, in theory, that the human and the shifter could work together, sharing their skills. It was just a case of finding the right people. No problem.

Marcus was probably the most important one to find, because he had led his team. Allegedly dead, but with evidence of his work to be found if one knew where to look. I enlisted the aid of both Bowman and Dragon, and eventually, the individual in agreed to a meeting at my apartment. The offices which I maintained were too public. I could understand that. I wanted this individual to agree to my proposal, so I was prepared to go out of my way to make him comfortable.

I had his military record, so I had more than just his name. When he arrived, I showed him through to the lounge area of the apartment. He accepted the offer of coffee.

"Feel free to sweep the room for any surveillance." I suggested, making my way to the kitchen. A ghost of a smile curved my guest's lips at the suggestion.

"Trust is always good." He replied. "You went to a lot of trouble to find me, so I am going to trust that you have something for me which you don't want me to turn down. Having surveillance devices installed is sure to make me suspicious." He accepted the mug of coffee, and took one of the armchairs. "So, I am going to trust that you wouldn't endanger my acceptance."

I didn't miss the slight wince as he sat down. An injury, likely from the ambush in which he was alleged to have died? Marcus himself confirmed as much, when I put my proposal to him.

"Helping troubled youth? Sounds interesting, particularly given the package you are offering. A real generous package for a washed-up Spec Ops like me." He was blunt. "So what else is involved? Washed-up I may be, but I ain't stupid."

"Washed-up? I doubt it. Not when certain individuals still speak of your skills." I replied. "I am looking for a specific calibre of individual. I believe that, if money is the motivator, then the package will be of sufficient interest. However, if you are the sort of person I believe, then I think the nature of the project will be of greater interest." Casimir leant back in his armchair. "Before we continue our discussion, let me make one thing clear to you. There is a lot at stake. I need this ... project to be successful. I will reveal confidential information to you, such that if you reveal what I tell you, to paraphrase Liam Neeson, I will find you and I will kill you." I smiled. "Are we clear?"

Marcus looked thoughtful. I had the impression that he was evaluating what he saw, both my own appearance and the apartment in which we were meeting. He took a slow drink of his coffee, before giving a small nod. "I trust my gut instinct, not least because the only time I didn't, I lost several members of my team in a desert.

From what Marcus and I had been able to determine, the pen-pusher who had been responsible for his team being dropped in what should have been a safe zone but had proved to be an ambush. Clearly he had not intended that any member of the team would survive. Damn shame for him then that whilst two had died, and two had been severely injured, their training had come through and they had made it back. Regardless of the threat, my gut tells me to trust you, so let's hear it. What is the unexpected factor that requires that level of caution?"

I smiled. "What I wish to establish is a bit more than a youth mentoring programme. In the course of my life to date, I have become somewhat adept at finding information, in places which are perhaps not so accessible to the authorities. I have also ferreted out information on individuals who may be described as lacking in morals. What I have found goes beyond what I need for my own business interests, but it still requires action to be taken. I want to build a team capable of taking that action, because there are situations when ..." I paused, knowing that this was the critical moment, "... human law enforcement cannot respond in an appropriate manner."

Marcus' eyes narrowed. He had picked up on what I had said, as I had never doubted that he would. "Human law enforcement? Care to clarify that?"

"It's quite simple." I allowed my eyes to take on the gold of my wolf. "I am not human. The so called troubled youngsters whom I wish to have mentored are not human. But, I want human mentors for a reason." I explained.

To his credit, Marcus did not leap up in surprise or react adversely. Instead, he took another slow drink from his mug of coffee.

"And what might that reason be?" He asked after a pause.

"In order to do what I envisage the youngsters need to be able to interact in a dangerous world. They need to be able to protect themselves. Those I intend to target are human in the main, but there is a risk of over-confidence because of … what we are." I explained to Marcus.

"So, you want a washed-up Spec Ops team leader to join your organisation?" Marcus chewed his lip for a moment. "I won't deny being interested. Being freelance lacks security, both financial and physical, and I am going to guess that because of whatever it might be that you are, you are security conscious in more ways that one."

Marcus cleared his throat. "So, I have a question for you. Does your … organisation have space for others with my sort of training?"

I smiled. "As in the other members of your team?" I asked. "Yes, I investigated. How many of your original team survived the ambush?"

The change in Marcus' expression was sudden. He went from thoughtful to bleak. "I lost three in that ambush. Should have trusted my gut. Something told me … but the higher ups gave us a mission go order."

"Do you believe that they would have a problem with the nature of my organisation?" I asked. After all, these were humans trained to kill. I was not going to expose young shifters to the risk of death at the hands of a human.

"My team were ambushed in circumstances which screamed set up. I lost three good SEALS that day. I couldn't stop to take their bodies because I would have lost more. Another of my team nearly lost his life that day. I had to use my skills to ensure that we could drop out of sight, so to add to it all, we are listed as fucking deserters. Trust me, we are too busy ensuring we stay alive and find the bastards who did this." Marcus had regained his earlier expression. "You said that you want us to mentor 'youth'. Kids, right? We don't kill kids." He almost spat the last words out.

I nodded. I believed him. "Then I believe we have a deal, Mr Jones."

Courtesy of one of the shell companies I used to hide my own money from my sire, I had ownership of a block or two of upmarket apartments. I gave Marcus the choice, and I explained that I was also building a home in the Catskills, some three hours away from New York City.

Marcus and Jon were two of them. The others, like Marcus and Jon, had suffered some form of injury. It had been a result of training and of sheer determination, the will to ensure that they didn't die in that hell-hole, which had meant that ten of them had survived. Three of them hadn't survived and that was part and parcel of the shadow I would see in Marcus' eyes. As the intel expert and team leader, he had held himself responsible for what had happened. He had tormented himself with the question of whether he had missed something in his analysis of their mission.

Why was this germane on the fact that the rooms being used by my new Pack? Marcus was wary of sudden noises; it was part of his PTSD. So, his room was soundproofed and equipped with white noise, so that he had just enough background noise to remind himself that he was alive, that he wasn't still stuck in some forsaken desert. When we were finally able to move to the property in the Catskills, and be the Pack that I had envisaged, I would watch him on occasion. Towards the evening, I would see him rub the outside edge of his left leg, a residual ache from the compound fracture he had sustained. That was when that distant look would appear in his eyes, and he would stop what he was doing, his mind dragged back to replaying that fatal mission.

More often than not, I would also see Marcus' young partner, Sarah-Jane, go to him. She would not say anything, but her slim hand would cover Marcus' larger paw, and they would just sit in silence. All she did was remind him that she was there. For a young shifter, she was remarkably perceptive when it came to her partner. She never pushed him. She never asked questions. She knew that when the time was right, he might be able to open up and talk about what had happened. Until then, she made it clear to him that she was there. Partners. Pack-mates.

When Marcus Aurelius Jones had taken the choice to disappear, it had not been willingly. But it had been determined that his injuries, which had left him with a slight limp, meant that he could not continue in the role for which he had been trained. There was also an element that it was easier to think that a 'troubled' former soldier might choose a particular way out of his change in circumstances. It happened. Suicide happened.

As a tech expert, had he wanted to leave the Teams, Marcus should have been able to find employment in a variety of private sector companies. Instead, he had had to use his skills to make his team disappear. He did a very through job. It just happened that I was better. That was how I found him. I use sources of information which are ... not the norm for the CEO and venture capitalist, but information is how my company chooses its projects.

CHAPTER 18 – THE FORMATION OF A PACK: BETH

Seeing the way that Jon and Beth worked together had reminded me of why I had been driven to try giving my blood to Daniela when she lay in a coma.

My Pack was in its relative infancy then. With the death of my sire, those of his lieutenants who could see that they would lose their 'privileges' under my brother, Adhémar, declared that they saw me as the true heir to the Gosselin Pack. In me, the acknowledged Psycho Gosselin, they saw one who would pick up the myriad of ... income streams which my sire had instigated, and which I had been ordered to help establish and conceal. I had concealed them, but it was with the intention that what I had constructed, I could destroy. Even then in my mind, those fuckers were slated to die, preferably with the same level of pain that they had meted out to their victims.

However, it was a lonely place to be. Perhaps that was why I saw Rosa Anastasia as an unattainable angel. Unattainable to one such as I, soiled from association with my sire and his 'advisors', soiled by what I had done in the name of protecting those who had no one else willing or capable of mitigating my sire's worse excesses. In Ma Petite, I found another like me, I thought, with a similar background, her soul wounded and scarred by what she had to survive. Together we started to help each other heal. Where that would lead, I didn't know.

But, back to the first time I met Jon Taylor. He had been introduced to me by Marcus, a former team member, who had also left the Armed Forces. However, unlike Marcus, Jon had little choice in the matter. Severe facial scarring left him virtually blind, able to distinguish dark and light and a vague shape if the light was strong enough, but that was it. Having joined my 'mentoring' programme a month beforehand, Marcus had learned of what I was really trying to achieve. Quartered in a secret apartment complex, he had set about tracking down his former team.

Jon Taylor was the first one he found.

How was it Martin Luther King Jnr put it? "I have a dream..." Sounds so cheesy coming from the Psycho Gosselin, but if the proverbial shoe fits ...

I laughed when I read those two lines. Introspection is not my strong point. I have hidden behind an image for too long. For that reason, in order to do what I felt was necessary, I had to start living a double life. I had my own wealth by the time my sire was killed, investments I had made through funds my bankers had released to me on my 21st birthday, funds which they said were from my mother's family. Who was I to argue? It was money which I could use to implement that 'dream', and that was all that mattered.

It meant that I could purchase property about which my sire knew nothing. I could have it built to my own specifications, presenting one image whilst concealing its true purpose. It meant that when my sire's lieutenants thought they were moving into my home, they saw but a fraction of the building's true purpose. Only a select few saw the rest, those whom I felt I could trust. It gave me space where I didn't have to hide who I was with a group of individuals who understood that sometimes the truth had to be concealed and they were more than capable of 'having my back'.

The crowning irony was that the Psycho Gosselin, the wolf shifter who was rumoured to kill without conscience, entrusted his secret to a group of humans.

When building my new home in the Catskills, one of the things of which I could take advantage was the discovery of what appeared to be old mining tunnels of some kind. I wasn't sure what they had mined, or how old the tunnels were. The key thing for me was that they were well and truly abandoned, and the entrances were overgrown, concealed from casual enquiries.

Why was this important? I was building an extensive underground complex in my new home, and I did not want my sire or later my sire's former lieutenants to know of it. Therefore, those members of my Pack who would have access via this route needed an entrance which was far enough that it would not be noted. The tunnels required work, no doubt about that, but the nett result was that I had my concealed access and exit points. With both of them requiring passage through a water source, it meant that even if my sire's lieutenants stumbled on it, the scents would be masked. If anything, the human scent around the tunnels would make it clear that there was no connection to the home of the Psycho heir to Pierre Gosselin, who made his scorn of 'human cattle' only too clear.

Beth was another early member of my Pack, so when Marcus introduced me to his former team mate, Jon Taylor, I had immediately considered whether she would be the ideal partner for him to mentor.

I had met Beth when I was allegedly out hiking. Truth be told, I had heard that there might be a shifter living out in the woods, and I was curious. I needed my new home to be secure, and if there was any risk, then yes, I would eliminate that risk. I had expected to find some grizzled old timer, who had enough of living in the city and was letting the wolf take over. I did not expect to find a shifter still in her teens, but with a very good reason to want to hide out in her wolf form, and not be bothered by people.

Beth had a ... well, you could call it a disability or you could call it an enhanced ability. Her hearing as a human was too acute, as well as her sense of smell. Her parents had insisted that she stay in human form, wanting to blend in with the world around them. Perish the thought that anyone discovered that they were shifters. Fair enough, since most of us did 'hide' our shifter nature except in our own homes. But Beth's parents had insisted that she maintain her human form even at home. If anything, they viewed being in wolf form as giving in to their baser natures, and they were 'better' than that.

So, as soon as Beth felt that she was old enough to survive in the wild, she ran. Her parents had called out the police, claiming that their daughter may have been abducted. Yes, I suppose you could argue that, because she had been 'abducted' by her animal nature. But she was able to survive and she was happy. No more voices to hammer her skull with their tones and frequencies. No pheromones or just plain odour to blast her sense of smell. Just the peace and tranquillity of the forests of the Catskill mountains. If the rangers ever thought that a wolf was a strange creature for the area, then she let them think that it was just a creature passing through.

Beth knew I was there, and her posture when she saw me reflected that she also knew I was an alpha male wolf shifter. She was standing on a rock ledge above me. Her form had shimmered slightly as she shifted back to her human form, to reveal what most would have taken to be a slightly grubby-looking and naked Caucasian teenager.

"I won't go back." She whispered. "You can't make me go back, please."

Wordlessly, I reached behind me to my pack, and pulled out a shirt, one of my own. Balling it up, I threw it up to her. She caught it, her surprise clear. "Join me down here, and we can talk." I suggested. "And I assure you, forcing you to do something which causes you such fear is the last thing I would do."

I folded my legs and dropped to the soft ground, waiting. It wasn't long before she joined me, her bare feet relatively soundless. I didn't move. She struck me as being as highly strung as a rabbit wanting to flee a predator or a trap, yet unable to resist the bait of the trap. She sat down opposite me, but her head and shoulders dipped again, an instinctive reaction.

"So, why don't you want to go back?" I asked her quietly, deliberately aiming to avoid spooking her. "You are young, and surely you would prefer the company of others your age?"

She shuddered. "I can't." She whispered. "I can't take their voices. My parents want me to stay human, but that means going to human high school and a human college." Her head dipped even more. "My hearing." The voice was so quiet, it was just as well I was a shifter. "My hearing is too acute. It hurts to be with people."

"What if I offered you an alternative?" I suggested. Beth looked up at me, a hint of hope in her face. She was lonely, there was no doubt there, but clearly thought that this was the only way she could avoid the pain from her 'disability'.

"I am building my Pack with a specific aim, but I need those I can trust, because what I want to do is not something that can be common knowledge." I explained. "It won't be just shifters." I pointed out. "There are things I want to do and your 'disability' will be very useful indeed. I know that much." I shrugged. "I can't say why I know it, but I did know that I had to find you, and convince you."

As Beth and I sat in that clearing, I explained to her the plans that I had for my Pack, the complexity that was involved. It stood to reason that to have a Pack member who 'owed' me something, who also happened to have a 'disability' which meant that she would overhear any plans being made by those who didn't share my vision. But, I didn't see convincing Beth in that light.

I was walking a fine line. On the one hand, I had to maintain the appearance of being the Psycho Gosselin, the true heir to Pierre Gosselin in terms of my ruthlessness and my drive to pursue those enterprises which benefited my view of the world. That was the impression that meant that my late sire's lieutenants flocked to my 'banner', so to speak. Mentally, I viewed them with scorn. They were followers. They were scared enough that they might lose the plush lifestyle they enjoyed under my sire that they would do pretty much anything to ensure that their little bubble was not burst. They disgusted me, make no mistake there.

My birth Pack was in the 'safe' hands of its new Alpha, my younger brother Adhémar Gosselin, but there were certain enterprises which were residues of my sire's activities, enterprises which I had helped him to establish. Those I wanted to take down. There would be no legacy of Pierre Gosselin. I was going to take great pleasure in wiping his name from the face of this world. But, I had to tread carefully. I was on my own, unless I could establish a Pack around me, and that was where individuals like Marcus Aurelius Jones and his former team members, where Beth and other young shifters like her came into play. They would form the true core of the 'Hellfire Pack'.

So, when Beth, with that burgeoning hope in her eyes that I might give her a way to enjoy the feeling of Pack, without having to conform to her parents' wishes, agreed to join me. I was more than pleased.

Opening my Pack, I extracted the full change of clothing which, for some inexplicable reason, I had added to my supplies for this hike. "Dress yourself properly, and I will take you to meet some of the others. After that, if you prefer to stay in your wolf form, that will be your choice."

When Beth accompanied me back to the apartment block I had purchased for the use of my true Pack, I made a point of explaining to her that the rooms had been heavily soundproofed. Part of that was to avoid the risk of my plans being overheard. A more important element was to ensure that my new Pack felt secure.

DIARIES OF THE CŴN ANNWN

CHAPTER 19 – AVIGAIL

"That lawyer needs to be dealt with. She's a danger to our interests. We will be a laughing stock if we let her have her way."

There was no question in how I was going to react to that statement, or to the individual who made it. One of my late sire's closest allies and there was also no doubt in why he had said what he did. From my relatively calm stance, of one arm resting on the mantelpiece of the fireplace in my study, the other hand holding a cut-crystal glass of an excellent Scottish single malt, I moved.

The glass shattered on the carpet as with a snarl, I grabbed the individual by the throat, my hand tightening, my smile demonstrating that the fact that he was scrabbling to release himself and draw breath was a source of pleasure to me. "Are you challenging how your Alpha chooses to act?" My voice was quiet, as befitted the sudden silence which had befallen the room. I released the hold I had on his throat just a tad, enough to allow him to draw breath. "Think very carefully on how you respond." As I released his throat completely, my other hand came into view, to reveal a knife which most of them had not even realised I carried. The point pressed against the back of his skull. One move and it would drive into his brain. "If you even think to challenge me, I have a simple solution for such idiocy." My smile was cold. "Think carefully." I reminded him.

The male's eyes met mine and he shook his head, before dropping his gaze. Falling to his knees, he made it clear to everyone else in the room that he was ceding to my authority, as he should, given that he claimed to have sworn allegiance to me as his Alpha.

"Yes, the lawyer is proving to be an issue. But think, *mes amis*. How would it look for her to die suddenly? Our contacts are in Vice. A murder is handled by Homicide, and with my dear sister working in that Department, do you really think that she will let a murder that potentially involves me to be investigated in a less than thorough manner?" I looked at the still kneeling male. "Clear up that glass before it ruins the carpet, and pour me a replacement." I snarled at him, casually closing the blade of the knife I carried still. "No, murder of the lawyer is anything but a solution. If anything, it risks bringing our activities and our links with the State Police, into the wider arena. Make no mistake, that would be sloppy indeed, and I would really be quite upset if any of you thought to act independently of your Alpha's instructions."

I made a point of meeting the eyes of each of the six males in the room, waiting until each one had dropped his gaze, clearly indicating their subservience to me. However, knowing the way that their minds worked, I knew I had to make arrangements regarding the lawyer, Avigail Micula. Why? I was not so stupid that I would believe that they wouldn't attempt to deal with the 'problem' she had posed with her extensive enquiries into the disappearances of young women both in the local area and further afield. How does the saying go? It is easier to seek forgiveness than gain permission. I had no doubts that unless I handled the problem myself, one of these numbskulls would take it upon themselves to determine whether that cliché would apply to me.

This was going to be a situation where I needed to use resources of which my alleged Pack remained unaware. It was true to say that those six males had accepted as their Alpha, as the 'heir' to my sire after he and Laurent were executed by the Cŵn Annwn. But, and this mattered to me, even if it did not matter to them, I did not consider them my Pack. It was to my true Pack that I went, so that we might find a way to protect Avigail Micula.

For all that I was trying to achieve, working with these remnants of my sire's Pack left me with a feeling of being soiled. When Avigail became my guest, that feeling was amplified. Who was Avigail Micula? Well, her background is covered elsewhere, but the fact was that a half-human female, born of IVF from a donated Cŵn Annwn gamete, was not going to be an ordinary female. That was the woman who was brought to the apartment I put aside for her. Fear would have been a perfectly normal reaction when your home is invaded by two masked and armed men, but if she was afraid, she made an excellent attempt to hide it. Her destination apartment was not registered as Pack property, but rather as the private residence of the other male who had accompanied me. Avigail had a grim look on her face as I injected her with a sedative, so that she would not be able to identify her destination. Other members of my true Pack attended to her needs, making a point of not conversing with her.

I could not risk that Avigail might identify either her location or her captors. If there was to be blame laid at anyone's door, then it would be mine. That is the role of an Alpha. Plus, I had a reason for Avigail linking me with her kidnap. I intended that she would 'escape' somehow, but when it happened, it had to be controlled, because make no mistake, Avigail would still be in danger from the loose cannons that were my late sire's followers. I had to be certain that she 'escaped' to somewhere where they would not be able to touch her. There was one individual I would trust, and he didn't even know who I was.

However, going back to Avigail's sojourn with me, I recall that I had a moment or two of weakness. Was it too much that I wanted the proximity of an individual as pure as Avigail? Was it wrong that I didn't wish to be so alone? Alpha I might be, a pack I might have, but when I went to sleep, it was on my own. I think that was why I was driven to spend time with Avigail. Even knowing, as I do now, that she could not have fought the physical reaction to me, at the time, I wanted to believe that her reaction was real, that someone as pure as Avigail might see someone with at least a small degree of worth. Live in association with such scum as I spent most of my time, and that even such a glimmer was priceless.

That sounds so pathetic, so plaintive. But at the time, those were the thoughts in my soul. I had chosen a course of action, one which my mentor had endorsed, but it was not an easy course. When the time came, my contact received the information that was needed to retrieve Avigail from my care. The matter was anything but closed. That project of my sire's creation had several strands which required termination. Whilst my inadvertent and unknowing allies might deal with some of those strands, there was one connection which was mine to terminate: the contact in the State Police Vice team.

<u>CHAPTER 20 – ANOTHER ONE BITES THE DUST</u>

There was an undeniable sense of satisfaction, as I looked at the faces of the gang members who had been involved in the kidnap of so many young college women. Human they may have been and thus according to my sire of little regard. But they were still individuals, they still had dreams, they still had hopes and what my sire had done to them was to destroy those hopes. Others have had dreams destroyed, but what my sire did to these women, the way he viewed them as commodities and little more than that, was aimed at one thing and one thing only. He wanted to see the knowledge in their eyes that it was over or at least that it would only be over when their so-called masters granted them that freedom, the freedom of death.

So yes, I was filled with satisfaction at being able to contribute to the destruction of a sex trafficking ring that not just covered the continental USA but spread worldwide. For some it was too late but for a small group, a small courageous group of women, assisted by those who saw me as the enemy, they could once more start to dream.

One of the first things I had to do was eliminate any gang members who had actually seen my face. That was fairly straightforward, since I had made a point of only meeting in person with whomever was leading them at the time. That was a neck snapped without any feelings of guilt. Let the authorities wonder how a prisoner in a locked cell had his neck broken. That did not matter to me.

Stage two of the process was to find a lawyer who would be given a very specific set of instructions, bearing in mind that I intended the gang to be found guilty. I had to ensure that they were not appointed a state-supplied defence team, who would do as was expected which was to try to exonerate their clients of any wrongdoing. Despite them being found on the premises where the girls were alleged to have been held, we were talking the human justice system did have to operate on the premise of innocent until proven guilty. Now I knew that the Cŵn Annwn were both alive and more than willing to involve themselves in the world, had the gang been shifters, they would have been read by the servants of Mallt-y-Nos and their souls harvested.

I wanted to ensure that whilst the gang's lawyer gave the impression of defending his clients, I made it clear that he was not to put the victims, the girls who had been rescued, through the sort of aggressive cross-examination that was seen all too often in sexual abuse cases. His brief was quite clear. The gang would be found guilty of all charges. They were guilty, but due human justice processes had to be observed. In the meantime, I needed to ensure that there was no hint that my own alleged actions were being investigated. The gang might talk of someone from whom they took orders, but there was no evidence of such an individual existing. There were still aspects of my late sire's business dealings which I was working to uncover. Swimming in that swill would not have been possible had there been a hint that the Psycho Gosselin was a fiction.

I know how the narrative of those events reads. I know there are things which I am alleged to have done. But, and this is key, I do not deny doing those things. I do not deny that I took a shot at Aaleahya Negrescu, potentially earning the lifelong enmity of her mate Gavril. I do not deny that I took a shot at my own brother-in-law. I knew that in doing so my sister would cement her hatred of me. But I had my reasons and those reasons were that I had more to accomplish. I was not ready to be accepted into the fold of good guys. I needed to remain on the outside. If for one moment my sister or my brother-in-law or any involved in the rescue of those kidnapped women had thought that I was playing a double game, I stood to lose much more. I was not prepared, not at that stage anyway, to take that gamble.

I would however like to put a couple of things in perspective. Remember if you will that I had a mentor in my uncle, Zarek Svitovidson. Why was this important? It was important for one key reason. My uncle was instrumental in the Negrescu twins being born, infants who shared a precognitive ability. This meant that particularly if my uncle so willed it, my actions, such as allegedly attempting to assassinate the Aaleahya Negrescu, would not succeed because the twins would give warning.

The same thing happened when I attempted to shoot my brother-in-law outside the courthouse. The instructions my uncle gave me were that I should aim for a heart shot. Given that my uncle was an associate of Gavril's Pack, that instruction might seem strange to an outsider. But remember the twins' ability. My uncle knew that Bran would be warned. Given that it wasn't the first time somebody had taken a shot at him he would move in a particular manner with the intent of preventing a successful heart shot. My uncle knew this which was why he felt confident telling me to aim for the heart. The shot would never succeed and more to the point an individual of Bran's age and ability, was able to heal himself of a clean bullet wound. The minor detail of his speedy healing was handled smoothly, so no one thought anything amiss. But it left the so-called good guys under the impression that the chief suspect, Casimir Gosselin, was prepared to take fairly extreme measures to protect his nefarious interests.

CHAPTER 21 – CADUCEUS

The roots of what was to become the so-called designer drug, developed to take advantage of the human physiology, had also started under my sire's rule. He claimed to encourage creativity amongst his followers. What could be more creative than a cross between Viagra and the high engendered from something like Ecstasy. Put the two together and surely you would have a winner. The problem for me was that such an attitude meant when those formerly lieutenants flocked to my banner after my sire was executed, they brought with them all the projects conceived under his rule and authorised by him. So, to their minds they were doing nothing wrong; their work had been authorised by their Alpha. Of course, I could hardly say to them that I intended to shut down the little pet projects and ensure that they paid for what they did. Had I done so that would have led to me being one of the shortest-lived Alphas in shifter history.

This was why, relatively early into taking over the dregs of my sire's pack, I found myself in Las Vegas, having ridden from New York on my Triumph Tiger Explorer. I could have used the Lear jet to travel down to Las Vegas since after all, it was kept at the Buffalo airfield for my own use. It had been one of the assets I had been able to secure when my brother had taken over the remnants of the Gosselin Pack. But had I used to the jet it would have alerted others to my intent not least because I would have had file a flight plan.

Riding the Tiger down to Las Vegas was the only practical option. No flight plan was needed. Those who needed to know my location knew how to find me but equally, those like my sister Alix, who would have just love to have me in her custody, would have to wait her turn. On the plus side, I had booked myself into an Indigo hotel: comfortable, but the chain hotel nonetheless, and certainly not the sort which anyone would expect me to use.

CYSGODION

My investigations had indicated that my target, one of my
sire's formerly tenants, was working from this affront to
wolves senses that was Las Vegas. I shuddered at the
recollection. Lights too bright, noise sufficient to make my
head pound, but then it was small wonder that aforementioned
lieutenant had felt he could work uninterrupted here since it
was so shifter unfriendly. Under my sire, the male had been
left to his own devices, but this was not a state of affairs
which I was prepared to allow to continue. The side-effects of
his little chemistry project were significant. And by
significant I meant users had died. Whilst my intention may
have been to shut down all remnants of my sire's business
empire, I had to do it in a controlled manner. Deaths amongst
users of this drug would have attracted law enforcement
interest, assuming of course that Detective Johnson and his ilk
did not manage to bury the information as they were paid to
do. It would appear that Las Vegas was being used as a test
site, prior to the drug being rolled out. But something told me
that usage amongst the general population, whilst likely to be
lucrative, was not the end intention for this drug.

Let me explain this. We are talking the drug which had the
effects of Viagra, insofar as it ensured libido was maintained.
It also resulted in the sort of uninhibited behaviour that was
often seen amongst users of ecstasy and other forms of
MDMA. Now combine those effects, with the fact that my
sire had set up a sex trafficking business. The customers of
that business were likely to be repeat business, since, as one
might put it, they had a tendency to break their toys. So
imagine if you will, a young woman kidnapped, sold into
slavery, where her owner would like nothing more than his
new possession to demonstrate her need for his attentions, and
need which would push her beyond physiological capability
and would lead to her death. Of course, her owner would
return to the business which provided him with such
entertainment. Thus my sire was ensuring repeat business.
The cycle of kidnap, of degradation, of slavery, of pain and

ultimately of death would ensure an almost never-ending source of income.

That was why it was essential that this little "chemistry project" was not allowed to succeed.

"No, you listen to me." On this matter I had to be the Alpha through and through. Any hint that I was prepared to give way to the scum, would have been seen as an immediate weakness. In this game weakness could meet my death. As the male on the other end of the phone continue to prattle I decided to interrupt him. "Clearly, you have an issue which now requires my personal attention." My voice was cold that it was sufficient for the male on the phone to realise that he might have pushed the boundaries.

"I do not need your permission to see the site where you are carrying out your clinical trials. I know where you are." The fool had been talking long enough that I had been able to triangulate his position. "Do not attempt to conceal what you have been doing. If you still have any live test subjects, I will see them." My fingers drummed on the table. "Based on my assessment of what I find, I will determine whether you will die sooner rather than later."

There was time enough to do a little bit more research on this project, given that what I had found so far showed that the individual behind the plan was both a chemistry minded genius and a risk aware ignoramus. Working my way through the various firewalls used was a bit like doing a fiendish sudoku puzzle for a human. It was a pleasant challenge and I had a half smile on my face as I worked my way through the various online barriers using one of my laptops while the other was researching the sources of ingredients which I have found to date. As I worked I was scribbling various notes, various permutations and implications of what I had discovered so far. Sitting back I had looked at my calculations. "If I could kill you myself, I would." I muttered, thinking if my late sire still lived I would have taken great pleasure in ending his life myself. The fool had not even considered the implications of approving this little project. If the human authorities had seized even a portion of the information that I had discovered, they would not bother to look further than the Gosselin businesses obviously involved. Breaking this down was going to take longer than I had thought, plus I had to ensure that the less savoury members of the law enforcement community did not hold any information of what they might think was the set up. There was a very real risk of blackmail, if they thought that their comfortable arrangements might be disrupted. If that happened there wouldn't be Gosselin Pack left, not even the good side under my brother, and that was just based on my having dug only part way through the information.

As with anything though, the fact was that as damning as the information I had discovered so far might appear, I needed physical proof of what had been done and whilst everything indicated that this individual had received his approval from my sire, I needed to make sure that he was not working alone. Six adult males had flocked to the banner of the so-called Psycho Gosselin, seeing me as the heir to everything which Pierre Gosselin had built. One of them was involved in this sordid affair. That much I had determined so far. But what I needed to ascertain was whether any of the remaining five were also in. Based on what I have found so far, they had done enough that my sire's fate should be their own.

But there were two in particular whom I wished would pay the full penalty of allowing themselves to be bought by my sire. One was the vice squad detective, Johnson. He was what people would term a media hound, or rather a media slut. Nothing gave him greater pleasure, it seemed, then seeing his picture splashed across the front pages because he had succeeded in yet another drug bust. The other individual whose perfidy I found particularly galling, perhaps because she worked for a government agency, a position which should have meant that her honesty was assured. It was anything but. Here's a feeling passed over by male colleagues, feeling that no matter how hard she worked it would serve little purpose since others would be promoted over her head. Agent Ann Burnett was her name, a fine officer the Federal Bureau of Investigation. And she was as bent as the proverbial rotten nail.

However, before I might deal with Detective Johnson and Agent Burnett, first I had to compile a more thorough dossier of what had happened to this little chemistry project since my sire had authorised it. Having triangulated the location of the male in charge of the project, I went in search of him. I had every expectation that he would try to conceal the most damning evidence of what he had done to date, but some of that evidence is impossible to conceal, particularly if one is an Alpha wolf shifter. Interestingly enough he had chosen to hide his operation in an office building. That actually made sense because it was far too much of a stereotype for the drug dealing operation to be hidden in some dingy warehouse, and after all, if one is making up a chemical product, in theory there should be some element of "good manufacturing practice".

Office building notwithstanding he could not hide the stench of dead bodies. Yes, if the authorities had searched the place, the human authorities that is, they would find no evidence of wrongdoing, because at least he had the sense to clean up sufficiently to satisfy their forensic procedures. He still had two live test subjects, both human, since after all that was his target clientele. He had one male and one female. The female had been restrained to a bed and whilst the padded restraints went some way to ensuring that she did not rub her wrists and ankles raw, the stench of repeated sex hung about the room. She writhed on that bed, her need, her desperation, apparent in her movements and in her tears. A queue of males waited by the door, some of them clearly clutching money, as they waited their turn to use the female test subject. If that description sounds dispassionate, it is because that is how I had to view it. Yes, somewhere that female may well have had friends or family who wondered where she had gone. But given how much of the compound had been administered, she was not long for this world. The male test subject fared little better. He had also been bound but his restraints varied slightly, so that he might service both male and female clients.

Yes, that former member of the Gosselin Pack, he was so proud of his set up. He was so proud that he was able to show me that he had perfected his drug, so he said, to ensure that the test subjects would survive sufficiently long to make the enterprise profitable. Then he pointed out, that as per his original brief from my sire, when he had deemed that the clinical trials had been successful, he had rolled out full production and full sale of the compound in question. This drug, this perversion, was now widely available along the eastern seaboard of the United States.

At least I did not have two soil myself with too many killings that afternoon. Both test subjects expired within an hour of my arrival, leaving a fair few disappointed potential clients. They had all left filing out of the building, no doubt certain that they would find amusement elsewhere. For my part I needed to shut down this cosy little set up. Again I cursed the name of my sire and wished that if Gavril had not already ended his pathetic life, that I might have been able to do so. The fact remained that even after I had killed the male in charge of this particular project, even after I had burned the sad remains of his two "clinical subjects", my work was anything but complete. What I had found here was only scraping the surface of the full situation. I needed to find out where and how this drug was being sold and I needed to do so quickly.

I had returned to my hotel room, in order to contact my true Pack, so that we might begin the process of tracking down where this compound was being sold, and ensuring that those best in a position to do something about it, had the information they needed. But as I said, how does one terminate an enterprise such as this, when the very individuals charged with protecting the human public, are the ones who seek to cause them harm for no other reason than it is financially profitable. To think that if the likes of Detective Johnson and Agent Burnett realised that I was not a human, they would call me an animal as if that would indicate that I was a lesser species. Yet they were the ones who failed to protect their own.

Of those touched by the spread of this particular enterprise, there was one to whom I had to present what had become my accepted face and make sure that both she and anyone else who happened to overhear believed what they both saw and heard.

It was not difficult to let others believe the worst of me. Perhaps that was what hurt the most. Alix? Well, I could understand why my sister would accept so easily that I was the mastermind behind this designer drug. She had the years of her life in the Gosselin Compound to reinforce the impression that she had.

By then, I had been contacted by a Demon, or at least he claimed to be a Demon. He said that he was in service to a Queen of Hell. He told me that his Queen had been betrayed. He claimed that she had been abandoned by the very creatures created to protect her. Hell hounds, that was how he described them. More to the point these hell hounds lived not that far from my own base of operations. In order to recover what she had lost, she appreciated the need for new allies and it was to this end that she had sent this Demon: to court to me, to convince me that it was in my interests to serve her or at least to work with her. I believe the human phrase here is "mamma didn't raise no fool". She was after all a Queen of Hell and anyone who believed that such an individual might be honest was deluding themselves in the extreme.

I had demanded proof of this Demon's abilities and by association of the Queen's sincerity. I had thought to make it slightly difficult so had requested that he bring me the assistant to the State police coroner. This human female, as I discovered, was the sister of the unfortunate male test subject I had encountered previously. I had not expected to find her on the floor of the entrance hall of my apartment but I realised when I did that I had to pretend that I intended to use her as a test subject, citing the fact that it would be interesting to see if the drug had the same effects on a female of the same genotype as the previous male test subject, her brother.

Slowly, but surely, I was working my way through the human involvement in this drug manufacturing and distribution network. But it was slow. I was playing a game of avoidance, whilst trying to confirm who had chosen instant wealth over their professed oaths to protect their fellow man. Let's face it, for an extensive drug distribution network to exist, there had to be law enforcement complicity. Detective Johnson was not the only one found to be accepting a retainer payment. His payment was greater because he acted as a recruiter for like-minded individuals through his professional network. Should I have found it amusing that he maintained meticulous records of individuals whom he had contacted? He had, and I would, in time, use that information myself. Those records were the proverbial axe which Johnson held over his co-conspirators.

I knew only too well that when, not if but when, this human female, Lily, was rescued, the situation would look damning indeed. I had spoken with my mentor, my uncle, and he had told me that more than I could possibly realise rested on this Demon and by association his Queen believing that I wished to play along with their games. He had spelled-out in graphic detail the potential consequences of my failing to convince them of my sincerity. There lay the conundrum. Part of me wanted to rail at my role in proceedings. When would it end? When might I be able to relax, to be 'me', rather than perpetuate this image?

What I did feel after Lily was rescued was that, if anything would seal my fate when I did allow Gavril to read my soul, I had felt that it would be what I had done to Lily. This one act, the way that I had condoned her abuse, and make no mistake it was abuse, meant that surely I had dammed my soul for eternity. I was no better than my late sire in that regard, in the way that I held humans as little more than livestock. I knew that is how others would view the situation.

Surely I must have wanted at some point to be allowed to argue why I acted in the way that I did, surely? But my uncle had made it clear to me that if there was even a hint that what I did was contrary to my own wishes and my own beliefs, then more than just a few humans would die. So I would ask you which is the lesser of the two evils. Do I let one person or maybe three die or do I risk that thousands might die? That was the choice presented to me. Believe me it was not an easy choice.

CHAPTER 22 – PLAYING WITH FIRE

If there was ever a time when I was playing with fire, it was when I became the public face of Lamashtu Anzillu, and when others realised that I might actually be working with their sworn enemy. On the face of it, it would look as if I had made a huge mistake. What did I, a mere wolf shifter, understand about working with a Sumerian Demon, a Demon who had existed long before the Christian version of God, long before the Muslim version of Allah. She had been there, in effect, from the dawn of civilisation, from the very early days when mankind built shelters for themselves and their gods, when they communicated with writing and the very concept of history and its potential came into being.

There was I. Nothing but a wolf shifter. So, what game was I playing? It was complex; there was no doubt there. What did I seek to achieve? Or rather should I say what did my uncle and I seek to achieve? Should I sound the fanfare? Surely such a major announcement requires some sort of acknowledgement? But it didn't at the time. At the time, just in the same way as I had "attempted" to shoot my brother-in-law or I had attempted to "assassinate" the mate of the Cwn Annwn Alpha, I wouldn't say I was playing a game but I was certainly acting out a role. I was playing with fire; there was no doubt in my mind about that. So, what do I mean?

As my uncle explained to me, there was a long term game plan in action. My grandsire had seen a time when humankind would fill what had for millennia been a sparsely inhabited world, and when that happened it would be inevitable that mankind would seek domination over others. It was very much a case of "nature of the beast". What humans failed to perceive was the little detail that in the same way as pagan gods and pagan pantheons had lost their power as the number of their worshippers declined, the same works in reverse. For some reason a line from the Christian Bible sprang to mind when I was thinking about this. Don't ask me to quote the exact chapter and verse, or even for that matter, in which of the four Gospels this particular line occurs. I think it is that bit where someone asks Jesus whether they should pay taxes to the Romans. The response is something along the lines of "give unto Caesar that which is Caesar's", said whilst holding a coin bearing the profile of the current Emperor of Rome. What that always meant to me was that since the coinage held the profile of the Emperor, it belonged to the Emperor. So why should this matter in terms of my grandsire's plans?

My grandsire is, not was, a god of warfare, fertility and divination. In the normal run of things, he would only have been worshipped in northern Europe. But at the beginning of the 20th century, there were two major conflicts in northern Europe or rather across the whole of Europe and a large portion of the world. Warfare. It mattered not who was fighting whom. All that mattered was that there was fighting and as gory as it might sound, land upon which blood has been spilt seems to have the tendency to grow and produce more productively the following seasons. Thus those major conflicts of the 20th century served to donate to at least two of my grandsire's attributes: war and fertility. However, what he had also seen was that there was a serious risk that these conflicts would not remain just in Europe or even in the so-called colonies of the European powers. War was fought for wealth and power. With the development of the internal combustion engine, oil became important and for some it became a resource to be coveted. It would be simplistic in the extreme for me to say that that was the only reason for war is occurring in the Middle East. However, what cannot be denied is the effect of those wars. In the same way that my grandsire was fed by the conflict that was World War I and World War II, so other powers started to stir as the level of conflict increased above their ancient seat of power, feeding them energy which might be nurtured and allowed to grow. And, as it grew, it generated more energy, more power.

Excuse me for a moment if I go slightly philosophical, but what would have happened if say, instead of marrying Lamashtu, the hunter had taken a more gentle deity as his bride? So much might have changed. My grandsire's plan would not have been needed.

But, that was not to be. The Hunter mated with Lamashtu, and then he put her aside, thus giving her the opportunity to nurture her hatred and her anger. It gave her the opportunity to formulate plans of her own, when perhaps she might even seek to destroy the Hunter.

I don't believe that Lamashtu honestly thought that Fane would ever leave her. After all she had identified his potential when he was still a juvenile. She had trained him, schooling him into the perfect Alpha for her. I doubt in all the years of her existence, that she did not think that Fane would take offence to her murder of his sister. Does the fact that I can understand how he might have been feeling mean anything in particular? No, it doesn't. Why do I feel that I could understand how both Fane and Lamashtu might have been feeling? It's quite simple. I would understand how Fane felt about his sister's murder because I felt exactly the same when Rosa was killed.

However, leave his former Queen? As extreme and wild an idea that it seemed to all around him, Fane did something completely different. Of course, now, we appreciate the impact that a relatively simple action might have. And yes, I do appreciate the joke, that had Fane not acted in the way that he did, we would have been facing a completely different outcome. He broke from his former Queen. He sealed the Pack's metaphysical loyalty to himself through the use of blood magic and that meant his Queen would not see the tiniest scrap of paranormal energy that he and his pack would raise. In deserting his former Queen, Fane earned her eternal hatred and yet, it might even be argued, it made him all the more desirable for having stood up to her. From that point on all that she wished to consider was to either kill him or to opt for the more merciful suggestion. Fane would never see it as a more merciful suggestion since it was simply a return to slavery for the whole of his pack.

If the state of Lamashtu's minions was a demonstration, then it was fair to say that Fane's former Queen took the news badly that he, or rather Stefania, would soon become parents. Fertility, the ability to have pups, was not something that she gave away likely since after all if the Alpha was to be intimate with another female for long enough that they might conceive a litter, it would be time spent away from her side, time when her Alpha, rather than protecting her and perhaps allowing her to satisfy her own lost on his body. It was not a gift which she would bestow lightly. When Stefania was brought to childbed and produced twin pups, again through messages relayed by her minions, her dismay and anger were communicated. Fail to interpret the situation appropriately and there would be just one individual to blame.

In the twins, Fane's former Queen found the perfect method to regain control over her Alpha, without damaging her or her home. Now, not only did Fane have pups of his own, but he did not keep them hidden unless danger threatened. To his former Queen this meant that he was mocking her.

They used to call it possession in the old days, when a demon might take over the body of some hapless human. That was the method which Lamashtu intended to use to wreak her revenge on Fane, only in her case, it was not a human whom she chose, but a member of Fane's own Pack, a female by the name of Sian. Why her? She had been the one to befriend the newly returned Stefania, before she became Fane's Mate. To Lamashtu, Sian was as guilty as Stefania of stealing Fane from her service. If she had not befriended Stefania, then the latter might have fled the Pack again. Fane would never have realised that Stefania was a lot more to him than just a Pack member. So, Sian became the target of her former Queen, a queen who more than adept at finding a deeply buried fears and insecurities and exploiting them. I must admit that I could not understand how she did not do the same to me, other than the additional protection granted me by my grandfather, because I was playing a pivotal role in his plans.

Sian's fear was that, because she had befriended Stefania, it demonstrated that she was less than a Hellhound ought to be. It did not help that there were still individuals within the Anghelescu Pack who were pushing against Fane's rule. By that, I mean Ivan Anghelescu. Watching from the side-lines as I was, I could not help but wonder why Fane put up with Ivan's thinly-veiled challenges to his authority. However, before I leap ahead in my narrative of events, there was that small matter of that first approach by the demon, and what had to be seen to happen in order to ensure that the longer-term plan.

It was essential, and I could not stress that enough, that the 'good guys' saw me as irretrievably evil. They had to believe that I had chosen to ally the scum remnants of my sire's Pack with the demoness, Lamashtu Anzillu. It had to be an unshakeable belief, because if Lamashtu had any hint that I was not as loyal as she thought, she would have snuffed my life in a blink. Why was it so essential? I had a street drug plot which I had to eliminate. My grandfather needed a spy on the inside. Harsh to think that I was a resource to be sacrificed? Well, that is life and that is war. Sacrifices might have to be made. There was a lure for me that one day, it might be 'over' and I could live my life for myself. And if I didn't survive? Well, I knew that Zarek would ensure that my Pack was protected, and it wasn't as if I had anything really to hold me to this world.

The demon intermediary had contacted me by text message initially, claiming to represent a party with whom I shared a common enemy. I had laughed on receiving the message. The gods knew I had more than a few individuals who thought that the world would do well to be rid of me.

[Text] *What's in it for me?* [End text] That much I did need to know. The reply came back surprisingly quickly.

[Text] *Power and revenge.* [End text]

Did I want to roll my eyes? That told me two things. The first was that the mystery caller was not a local, and secondly, they were old. That whole 'power and revenge' gig might have worked five hundred years ago, but as the saying goes, if you seek the path of revenge, best dig two graves.

[Text] *Revenge generally leads to two graves* [End text]

[Text] *Meet at co-ordinates to follow. Low risk to you.* [End text]

I needed this individual to prove themselves first.

[Text] *First prove yourself. There is a morgue technician asking difficult questions. I want her.* [End text]

If Jestan, the demon in question, thought that I was that daft to turn up at a meeting of this nature without backup, more fool him, particularly when I checked the co-ordinates and it was remarkably close to the mansion which had been bought by the group I had suspected were Cŵn Annwn, even before my sire's execution.

The members of my 'true' Pack were my backup, of course, both shifters and humans. Both groups were experienced enough that they knew to allow for wind conditions to ensure that they were not detected by the Cŵn Annwn. Jestan appeared from behind a tree, his form human. He raised a finger to his lips and gestured that I should crouch down, hiding behind the extensive undergrowth.

"Wait and watch, Casimir Gosselin." The demon hissed at me.

Fucking idiot, I thought. Thanks for using my name, potentially within earshot of the 'good guys'. Was he trying to cause trouble? Before I could say anything, there was a howl of rage, the slightly higher tone indicating that it came from a female throat. Jestan fell backwards as the attack from a shifter form seemed to take him by surprise. My brain registered Hellhound, but whoever it was, they had not transformed completely. The form shifted to reveal the, very naked, form of Stefania Anghelescu. A long dagger appeared in each hand. I make it a policy of mine to never underestimate the 'weaker sex' and Stefania's attack on Jestan was an excellent example of why. Her rage as she laid into him was apparent. He did succeed in drawing her blood, but it was a minor injury, from what I could see. When Stefania ripped out Jestan's tongue, it became quite clear that Jestan was not going to be winning this fight. Certainly, the ferocity with which Stefania fought should give anyone pause for thought.

I heard the howls of others, not my own Pack, and decided that it was high time for me to make myself scarce. Jestan was not going to be in a position to discuss anything. Whatever it was that was so important would have to wait. Still, when I arrived back at my apartment, it was to find Lily, bound and gagged. Not quite gift wrapped, but the message was clear. Jestan had fulfilled his side of the bargain. The question remained was what this mystery ally wanted from me in return.

CHAPTER 23 – ROSA AND DANIELA

I was clear in my own mind what I wished to build as my Pack. Marcus had coined a name for it, which caused much amusement both with his team and with the wolf shifters who had joined us by then. The Hellfire Pack. Why such a name? Two reasons. The first was that it had a decent touch of menace to it. After all, this was the Pack of Casimir Gosselin, the so-called Psycho Gosselin. The true reason was that hellfire in some form was probably what awaited us if our enemies ever guessed the truth.

Melodramatic much? No more than my thoughts on Avigail Micula, with her purity of character which seemed so untouchable. Since I had killed my one-time mentor in the Ring at the age of twelve, I had killed others. But each killing took something from me, or at least that was how it seemed to me. Avigail was purity personified, it seemed to me. A young woman who had dedicated her life to helping others, even when my sire and his former lieutenants threatened her, she had fought constantly for those who not have had a voice otherwise.

Rosa Anastasia was from a completely different mould. To start, she was a scion of the Anastasia family, which included the mobster known as The Executioner. It doesn't require the brains of Einstein to understand what he did for amusement. He was also well known for having been executed himself, whilst having his hair cut. His great-granddaughter had learnt from his mistakes. If you knew where to look, she had quite the reputation as a 'wet-work asset', but the other interesting thing was her visible business: an art gallery in a decent location, one which hosted soirees and exhibitions attracting the cream of society. It brought a smile to my face when I considered how many of those individuals realised that they saw but one side of Rosa Anastasia at those elegant evenings.

Ma Petite Psycho I would call her, a term of some affection, but at the same time, it was an acknowledgement of what Daniela Echeverria was in truth. A scion of the Spanish equivalent of the Mafia, she had allied herself with the Italian Cosa Nostra before emigrating to the USA, and setting herself up as one of the pre-eminent 'wet work assets' in the business of death. Given the direction of my activities, I had tasked my Beta, Rosa Anastasia, with bringing promising candidates to my attention, and Daniela was one such candidate. Rosa had used such a novel way to communicate her message: an arrow bearing a message tube, embedded in the wall of Daniela's apartment.

As instructed, Daniela presented herself at the apartment which I maintained in New York. Until I was certain of her, or at least as certain as one might be of someone like her, this was all she would see of me and mine. Slim built, with an affectation for heel-less boots. It made her seem smaller than she was perhaps, and I had no doubt that it was a trick that she used to make herself seem less of a threat if circumstances meant that she had to kill close-up.

That first time that Daniela encountered me in the gym in a pack house, she had seen what most saw on first meeting me. What harm could a relatively young looking male do, when he did not even look more than 30 years old? I can still recall her face when she realised that I was anything but a relatively young looking human male. Even at that stage there had been a fascination in her eyes, as she had done the proverbial maths, and worked out that the large lupine creature that she had observed through the windows, was that same "relatively young looking human male".

But, at that point, Daniela was nothing more than another member of my pack. She had been brought on board for the sole reason that she was a skilled assassin. She was known as one of the best "wet work assets" in the business. Having her on board meant that we were able to address certain inequalities in terms of far from satisfactory behaviour amongst the dregs of human society. Ethics had amused me, when she told me that she had no wish to be sent against those whom she had under her own protection. I had told her the same applied in reverse, that there were those under my own protection and I would be most displeased if she accepted a contract on any of them.

Daniela. A psychopath in a wrapper of normal was how I described her. I would wonder afterwards, was she truly a psychopath or like me, was she the product of circumstances? Had she also been forced to become something else through the actions of others? Should you think that my last comment meant that I blamed the actions of others for the type of mail that I had become, I would make it clear that I blame no others for my actions. I did what I felt I had to do at the time or as was the case with young Lily, I made a choice based on the available information. I had already made my decision and I wondered if Daniela had made a similar decision: better that one or two died than thousands.

CHAPTER 24 – DEATH OF AN ANGEL

I had been filled with a sense of foreboding when I spoke to Rosa. I could not help but recall that morning when Lamashtu had first appeared at my apartment in the body of another hell hound. I could not help but recall the threat she had made to Rosa. My instincts were screaming at me that this sudden contact by someone offering her information was just a little bit too coincidental. The gods know I have said often enough coincidences suck. But the problem was that Rosa was human and whilst she might appreciate that I was a wolf shifter, she did not truly appreciate our world. She had been raised in a monotheistic religion, Christianity or to be more precise Roman Catholicism. The concept of an ancient Sumerian Demon somehow being a threat to her personally would not be one that she would grasp easily but more importantly she would not appreciate that our enemy could adopt any appearance and there would be no telling who she was until potentially it was too late. So I had to fudge the situation, and not tell Rosa the risk. That was my mistake and it is a mistake with which I must live for the rest of my days.

When Lamashtu Anzillu killed Rosa, I knew that she had waited until I entered the bar and saw her sitting next to Rosa. She wanted me to know who had killed my Pack Beta. She wanted me to feel the guilt and the helplessness that I could not stop her. And damn her but she succeeded. It is never easy to admit that your enemy can read you that easily.

But Rosa's death also had another significant impact, and that was what I was willing to do in order that her spirit might find its rest. I was willing to risk death myself. Was that the result of the guilt which my enemy wanted me to feel? Quite probably. But equally, it was something that was a long time coming. I'm sure it could be argued that I should not have chosen helping the spirit of the pack mate over continuing to lead the living members of my pack. This is why it is so difficult to comment on recent events. My enemy wanted me to feel guilty and she succeeded without a doubt. That guilt drove me to make the phone call to the Alpha of the Cŵn Annwn. Guilt may have driven me to make that phone call, but I suspect my own subconscious wanted that judgement, and wanted to know whether I was damned through my past actions or was some part of me worth saving. Again, it is difficult for me to say this because honestly, my mind was in such turmoil that I could not have said what was the correct course of action. I suggest you judge that for yourself.

When it came down to it, Rosa was dead, my soul had been judged if not innocent then certainly not worthy of death, and I was able to acknowledge that as much as I would have liked to allow myself to have a relationship with Rosa it was not to be, not least because another had a far greater significance in my life. That other was the human assassin Daniela.

CHAPTER 25 – FINDING A MATE

I could not deny that there was something between Daniela and me. After she had been attacked, and after I had gone to her aid, in response to her mental call to me, I had insisted that she be placed on life support. There had been my anger at the suggestion that I should leave her die, rather than force her body to be kept alive by machines. There had been the way that I had taken to visiting her daily, talking to her, touching her face, holding her hands. I had been almost as if I was willing her to live. Those times I spent in her room, I had revealed a vulnerability which I had not wanted to show to anyone. There is a cliché: it is lonely at the top. Indeed it is, for an Alpha without a mate. Who would want to be the Mate of the Psycho Gosselin? But all that was moot as I would talk to Daniela, wanting her to respond to the sound of my voice.

Then came the day that I decided to try to bring her back through giving her my blood. It was known that humans could be turned with a bite, but would it bring her back? Had her brain suffered too much trauma? Again, I did not know, but I wanted to believe that ma Petite Psycho would return to me.

But, bringing Daniela out of the coma was only part of the story. There was much more before I realised why she was so important to me. I had made the decision to ask Gavril to judge my soul, knowing that, if he deemed me guilty, then his touch could kill me, harvest my soul and send me to pay for what I had done whilst alive. The relief I felt on being found, if not innocent, then certainly not worthy of immediate execution was indescribable. Did I think that the price of asking the Cwn Annwn to help Rosa would be my life? Yes. I did. I felt that I had done Rosa a disservice when she had lived, serving as my Pack Beta, as well as assisting me in matters which made little sense to her.

I recall the day when I had gone to the assistance of Fane's Pack, to protect his Mate, Stefania, from bounty hunters sent by Lamashtu. In theory, at the time, I was still working with Lamashtu, at least as far as my enemies were concerned. But I had other intentions behind my apparent alliance with Lamashtu. By then, my profile was such that it seemed logical I would work with her. She wanted to think that the new powers which I was demonstrating were through her 'benevolence'. The truth was that they were a direct result of my bloodline. The key thing was that the events involving Fane having to surrender himself to Lamashtu in exchange for his son served a key purpose, and that purpose required Stefania to remain safe. Rosa had not hesitated when I had told her I needed her help, even though it made little sense to her that I might help my enemy.

With that level of loyalty, how could I not try every option open to me to help spirit find peace after her death. If that meant my death, then so be it.

But, it didn't mean my death. What it did mean was that I received a timely reminder of what is important in life. I had failed to show Rosa how much she meant to me. I would not make that same mistake with ma Petite Psycho.

How did Daniela view the sudden news that I believed her to be my Mate? She had had only one shift to her wolf form, and that had not been a pleasant experience. Behaviours, which the shifter-born of my pack and I took for granted, were all strange to her. She had been a loner since she had left the not-to-tender care of her own family. Yet now, she found herself thrust into a pack. She found herself the lowest ranked member of that pack, by dint of being newly turned. That had not sat well with her. She didn't understand the nuances of wolf behaviour, for all that she had been living with shifters for several months. Then again, how many humans take the time to study wolves?

The most important aspect for me of discovering that I had a mate, something which I had genuinely believed would never happen, was the possibility that I might sire a young my own. Again I need to put this into context. Living in Janice's house I had believed that my own mother was dead. In effect, apart from those initial six years, Janice became the only mother figure that I had in my life. It would be fair to say that I did not have a particularly pleasant childhood. Growing up in a home where one parent abuses the other on a regular basis, and when the abused parent does not or cannot fight back, is not a method guaranteed to demonstrate parenting skills. As time passed, my memories of the first six years of my life when I had lived with my own mother, my own blood mother, seemed to fade, so the only thing, the only way I could learn about parenting was in watching my sire and Janice.

Then to discover that I could be a father myself? It was an emotional rollercoaster, to be blunt. There was that whole question of nature versus nurture. Would it be fair to bring Young into a world where the sire had known only abuse and likewise the dam because make no mistake Daniela's own upbringing was hardly a sterling example of parenting skills. There was the frisson of fear that I had felt from Daniela when the question of young was raised. I wanted to believe that I would not be the same sort of father that my own sire had been but I had no way of knowing. In the face of my own uncertainty, would it be fair on my mate? Would it be fair on any child that we might produce? So many questions. So few answers. It was ironic really that I was the grandson of a god of divination and yet on this aspect of my own future I had absolutely no idea what might happen or what I might do. What I do know is that when I did meet my niece, the child which Alex and Bran produced between them, it opened a part of me which I didn't even know existed. But more of that later.

Yes, that first moon run and Daniela's first experience of the meaning of being pack under a full moon; it had not been the best experience for her. I had no choice but to discipline her because she had to learn the hard way and that seemed wrong but if I had not acted the way that I did, she would not have understood that sometimes I had to be the pack Alpha, and not her lover. But her lover wanted her to understand, wanted her to realise that I had hated needing to discipline her in such a public manner. I don't know if this is something that a non-wolf shifter could actually understand. I am not sure I understand it myself given that I am trying to explain this and making a complete and total mess of it I suspect.

I suppose the key thing about finding a mate was that Daniela represented hope. She represented the possibility that the Psycho Gosselin might be laid to rest, consigned to history, because believe me I wanted nothing more than to leave that part of me behind. There you have it my foolish dream: being mated, having young of my own. Even the Psycho Gosselin should have a chance to dream.

CYSGODION

CHAPTER 26 – TRUTH AND FICTION

I call her "ma Petite Psycho". My life was 'organised'. I knew what I wished to achieve both for my own Pack and I terms of destroying any vestiges of my bastard sire's 'legacy'. Then, one day, Rosa Anastasia introduced a new potential member of my organisation, a female who specialised in assassination, who had made a name for herself both with the Italian Cosa Nostra and their Spanish counterparts, from whence she had been spawned.

She challenged me. She refused to accept my authority, both as a human and then, later, as a wolf created from my own blood. But, there was one very telling detail. That day that she was attacked, she called me, as a member of my Pack, and as much more than that. Three words: "I am sorry." That was all she said.

It had been enough. It was a clarion call, of more than a member of my Pack to her Alpha. I didn't know it then, but it was the call of my Mate. I could not have refused to answer had I even tried.

And now? Only the Goddess knows where our paths will take us. Would I change a moment of it? As I said to her, everything that has happened, our childhoods and the experiences of life has resulted in my having my Mate at my side.

If I had to live through it all again, I would not change a second, for that simple reason. Through those trials, I have my Daniela at my side. The price has been more than worth it.

CHAPTER 27: MEMOIRS – WHOSE BRILLIANT IDEA WAS THIS?

It had seemed like a good idea at the time, I told myself. Re-examine what had happened in my youth. How had it changed me, formed me, made me into the Psycho Gosselin, the hated and feared second son of Pierre Gosselin. Was being a psychopath part of my nature, or was it the result of 'nurture', and the way I had been raised? Then there were the thoughts of how my actions had affected others. Adhémar and I were slowly coming to terms with what had happened, but it was a work in progress, and then some. My sister Alix was a different matter.

Since that fateful night when Gavril had read my soul and then taken it upon himself to tell Alix what he had discovered, nothing had been the 'same'. Was the 'same' what I wanted? I had told Janice that I was more than happy for both Adhémar and Alix to hate me. I had said that I could live with their hatred, since it enabled me to be free to act on other matters. But had that been the truth? That was why I was sitting in his office, drumming my fingers on his desk, waiting. Elizabeth, my assistant, was out for an extended lunch, at my suggestion, although before she had gone, she had arranged for a 'business lunch' to be sent up to my office. For the sort of matters Alix and I needed to discuss, it was best that none overheard.

But where did one start. Perhaps that Christmas, when she had only been attending Miss Porter's for a scant school term. As the pack supposedly celebrated the mating of Laurent Gosselin and Christelle Bouchard, Janice and I had been determining a way to avoid Alix being mated off early for their sire's benefit. It had been the events surrounding them which had stuck in my mind, tainting Alix's recollection of me. I had been the bastard who had relished beating my young half-brother. I had spoken harsh truths to her about her role as far as our sire was concerned, intimating that even if she was mated early, the mating would only last for as long as our sire wished and that I would be the one to ensure her mate encountered a 'terminal event'. I claimed she might be mated repeatedly, forced to bear pups before she was herself out of childhood, all for the greater advancement of Pierre Gosselin. Yet, unknown to my sister, Janice and I had been laying plans, trying to find a way to ensure that Alix would be able to attend school and college and avoid the fate her sire had planned for her.

The phone on my desk rang, and the receptionist informed me that Detective Gosselin had arrived. Mind you, she was now a member of the JATTF. "Send her up." I ordered, and waited. Life was hectic now for Alix with her new position and responsibilities. Her time was assigned to a variety of projects and rarely did Alix have what people referred as 'free time,' but when her brother Casimir had asked her to come to his office and meet up, Alix moved her schedule around to go see him.

Even though she now knew that her heretofore hated brother had orchestrated everything to keep her dam and younger brother safe, not to mention the fact that I had been instrumental in saving Alix from the bleak fate for which her sire had deemed her good, I suspected the anxiety of just being in my presence had not diminished. All in all, it would be hard for Alix to stop this angst every time she came close to me, given our history. I knew that, thanks to her mating with Bran, she would appreciate that the past should be forgiven and forgotten, but how do you fight so many years of verbal abuse, the rift that had grown and filled with mistrust and hatred. Bran had assured me that he was helping my sister overcome her anxiety, but it was not going to be a rapid process.

Hearing Alix's voice, I stood, walking around the desk even as I acknowledged that I was wasting time, and trying to delay speaking with my sister. I laughed ruefully to myself. At least

I could now call her that, rather than any of the epithets our sire and Laurent preferred to use. Opening the door, I beckoned Alix in with a half-smile. "Welcome to my parlour, said the spider to the fly." I murmured. I indicated the lunch which awaited on the table near the sofa and chairs, the less formal side of my office. "Take a seat, and please, help yourself to some lunch. I think Elizabeth ordered enough to feed my Pack, rather than just two individuals." I half-joked, in an attempt to relieve the tension.

I could not help but be aware of Alix's tension. I had told Bran of my intention to meet with Alix, and my old friend had assured me that he would be 'listening in' on their Mating Bond, and would reassure Alix if he believed that she was becoming too nervous.

Taking a seat myself, I half-smiled again. "I was just browsing potential Yuletide gifts for my niece." I commented. "I just know what my Facebook 'targeted advertising' will have now." My smile was a bit wider. A newsfeed filled with pink bows and arrows was the least of my problems.

Alix snickered to herself, and I suspected that she could hear Bran laughing as he heard what she had heard. Bran was also feeding me relevant information. How could I have survived all these years knowing the loathing she had accumulated for me? How could Casimir even stand being around her? Alix had not made things easy for him while growing up in the Gosselin Mansion. She was just as stubborn as her sire. A shiver ran through her as Alix remembered the words they had exchanged that night during the Christmas party when Christelle and Laurent's mating was announced. To her mind, her dear brother, Casimir, was about to punish Adhémar for some obscure ridiculous reason, no doubt her sire's request.

As soon as I mentioned Kati Eliana, Alix's shoulders relaxed. This was our common ground. With a warm smile, Alix remembered the day Kati Eliana met her uncle and how she had asked to be picked up. My niece had reacted with the simple trust of a child, cutting through the mistrust and yes, hatred that had clouded my relationships with the adults present.

"Oh my, I can see it now…Princess parties, unicorns, pink tutus. Bless you! I feel your pain. Kati's bunny is starting to show signs of age." At least Alix had decided to give me a hint.

Helping myself to a selection of food, I half wondered if Alix thought subconsciously that I had tampered with the food in some way, something which would have been entirely in keeping with the Psycho Gosselin. Mentally, I shrugged. It would take time. I knew this. I felt a pulse of support through my own Mating Bond with Daniela. "Let them see the real you", the pulse said. Easier said than done.

I half-smiled again at my sister's unsubtle comment about Kati-Eliana's toy bunny. For this, I would even brave the horrors of the Hamley's soft toy department, if a replacement was required. It was little enough and not something I wished to leave to the anonymity of online shopping.

"Smiling." My lips twitched. "Not the easiest thing in the world ... sister." I commented. "People tend to wonder why I am smiling, given my reputation, and most assume that I am about to gut them either figuratively or in actuality." Pouring myself some coffee, I took a sip, before continuing. "I had nothing nefarious planned, Alix." I couldn't help but be aware of the small signs of tension. Years of verbal and mental abuse would have that effect, and it was not something that could vanish in an instant, regardless of the support that her Mate, Bran, was providing.

"I have been thinking, past events, why things happened. Do you remember that Christmas, just after you started at Miss Porter's?" I took another sip of coffee, as much to try to gather his thoughts. Casimir could recall only too clearly the image I had to leave both with Adhémar, of a beating at the hands of his elder brother, and with Alix, of my pleasure in administering the beating along with my scathing comments about her breeding potential. "I hoped you might want to know what was not so obvious when our sire was celebrating the union of the Bouchard and Gosselin Packs with Laurent's mating to Christelle Bouchard?"

 Alix could tell that I was trying. The road to healing this relationship was going to be a long one; she had no doubt of this. The plate of food stood there untouched, as she simply was too nervous to eat. When I attempted to smile, Alix smiled. She had to agree with me. I did look like he was conjuring an evil plan.

"Yes, I must agree with them. Your smile is nefarious, but I do know of someone that will never shy from it. Perhaps you should practice on her more often. Don't be a stranger, Kati Eliana asks for you often." Giving up on the food, Alix set the plate aside. She served herself some water and began to take little sips, smelling it first. It was ludicrous to think that I would go through all this trouble to poison her but old habits die hard.

"I would like to say the Christmas party is a fond memory but it is not, I still remember the sound of your belt." I had no way of being sure that she didn't mean to sound reproachful, but Adhémar had suffered so much at my hand, and Alix had been unable to do anything to stop the abuse.

She nodded "Yes, I would like to know. I am still in the dark about many things, but I know they will be revealed in due time." She waved me off to begin my recollection of that night.

I could remember the sound of my belt striking my younger brother only too well. "Well, for starters, you recall that your dam was in the room with me?" At Alix's nod, I continued. "Our sire had suggested that he might accept one of several offers made for you that night." My lip curled in disgust. "You were barely past puberty, but he could have done it, claimed you were homesick, and pulled you from Miss Porter's." I took another sip of my coffee. "I had to ensure that no one would disturb your dam and me in Adhémar's room. "Yes, I did hit him, but only once. I ensured he was unconscious so he didn't know what had transpired, but your dam will confirm it."

"I told our sire that one of our silent business partners had established a college fund for you. I used money from my inheritance from my own dam, money about which our sire knew nothing. It meant that he wouldn't risk angering a business partner by pulling you from school, no matter how advantageous the proposed mating might be."

Even this many years on, I could not help the growl in my voice. "The bastard broke Janice's cheekbone that evening. Neither of us wanted to risk him giving you to a potentially abusive spouse. But we had to ensure you and Adhémar knew nothing of what we had planned."

She nodded, as she remembered her dam with the bruise on her side. They hardly spoke back then, so this was also new to Alix. Her Maman had stood up to her sire that night, she had paid for that. Alix bowed her head, so much information filtering, consequences that could've happened. What would be her reaction?

Taking another big gulp of water, she couldn't help to say "Why did you have to hit him? He suffered so much. You could've hit me. I was strong, even then." She could hear the anger in my voice no doubt. I could almost see the processing in her mind. Was it possible that I loved Janice as a mother? Alix was still having issues with that. Their relationship was improving, but it would be a long time before they had mother daughter outings.

"I wouldn't want you to think me some sort of altruistic hero." My voice held a sardonic tone. "Why hit Adhémar and not you? Even then, I knew that I was not likely to be Alpha of the Gosselin Pack. It was always intended for Adhémar. But, he had to survive. He had the choice of our sire's wrath being delivered either by him in person or Laurent, which would have led to his death, or being delivered by me, which gave him his life, even if it was a life of painful memories."

I refreshed my own coffee, as much to give myself a mental 'breathing space'. Taking a long, thoughtful sip, I replaced the cup on the table. "Both of you had to believe that I was our sire's loyal second son. Our sire had to believe that if he ordered a punishment or a reprimand to be delivered at my hands, then it would be delivered, and the recipient would see the error of their ways."

I gave a harsh bark of laughter. "The exceptions were the bastards whom I killed in the fighting ring. Those deaths gave me much satisfaction. However, if there was a hint that I was playing our sire, do you think he would have let me live? You wore your heart on your sleeve, most of the time. Perhaps seeing how a 'family' should operate when you were at school gave you an understanding of how wrong things were at 'home'. The smallest slip from you or Adhémar and I would have died. Better that you saw me as a bully and hated me. More importantly, better you showed me how much you hated me." I smiled, hoping she could see the regret there. "I was starting to build my own pack, individuals whom I could trust. But I needed your hatred and I needed Adhémar's clear fear of me. Too many others needed some buffer between them and our sire."

The food must have looked like an appealing distraction, so standing she went to serve herself a plate. There was a lot to consider in my words, the assumptions she had lived with all her life were crumbling down. Sitting back again, Alix nibbled at a few things. She was stalling for time. Her words needed to come out a certain way. For now this meeting needed to be productive and positive. Alix knew this must not be easy for me. To show that I had a 'heart' after all and that in my own special way I actually cared for my brother and dam was something to admire. But, equally, I could see that she was not yet ready to believe I held any sort of fuzzy warm feeling towards her. Our animosity for each other spread throughout years was not something that was going to change any time soon. It was much easier for Alix to believe that I cared for her family and so, straightening her shoulders, she operated on that premise.

"I suppose you did the best you could with the circumstances that were handed to you. The scars would've been much worse if what you say would happen if you had been found out had come to fruition." My sister seemed certain that I had stuck my neck out, but why? "I guess the hardest thing I am finding believing is why would you protect us? What was your motivation?" She looked at me intently waiting for my answer.

I gave a bark of laughter. "Damned if I know." I brushed off the suggestion that some softer emotion might have been involved in my actions. I knew, from my discussions with my own dam, that my motivation had been my instincts from her side of my bloodline. However, how did I explain something like that to my sister.

"Maybe I have an idea now, but then? All I knew was that it was ... something I had to do." I paused, taking a further sip of my own coffee, grimacing slightly now that it had cooled down. "Then, all I knew was that there were some things I had to do. Let's face it, what eight-year-old in their right mind would challenge an adult male known for a fondness of his fists over his diktat that females should be culled at birth? But I did, and he listened. Now, I might attribute it to the fact that I have an element of divination from my bloodline."

I shrugged again. "That was when Janice, your dam, and I first started to work together. Remember, she was an Alpha's daughter, but she had no allies. Even an eight-year-old bastard was welcome as an ally." I was referring to the fact that my own dam had not been mated to Pierre Gosselin, something for which I thanked the gods. I smiled at the sudden memory. "The first time I was able to help reduce the impact of our sire's fists on her was also unexpected. Neither of us knew why I felt the need to touch her face, where he had split her lip, but when I did, it felt like a tingle of electricity, and the bleeding stopped."

"Janice explained to me when first you and then Adhémar were born that I could never inherit the Gosselin Pack, and strangely enough it didn't bother me. Perhaps I knew again, instinctively, that I would establish my own Pack, even if I would never have guessed at the time who would be in that Pack." Casimir stood to replenish the coffee in his cup.

"I appreciate your candour Casimir, this...whatever this is had helped me reconcile some irregularities in what I witnessed. Of course, back then I simply dismissed them. It was so much easier to hate you back then, than to fathom an ulterior motive for your actions."

Alix took her plate and nibbled some more as she saw me standing to refresh his cup of java. Alix tapped my shoulder. "What you did, for whatever motive was brave. The route you chose was crafty and filled with danger, but somehow you made it work. Thank you... thank you Casimir for helping my dam and my young brother. Thank you for preventing my future to be a sombre one."

Her words were but a whisper, but Alix knew I had heard every word. Looking up to me, her brows furrowed "What now?" The most difficult part about this discussion with my sister was that even now, even as adults, there were things which I knew, and I could not discuss. I understood fully the same dichotomy faced by my uncle, Zarek Svitovidson. There were matters which had to be permitted to play out, without inadvertent clues being dropped.

"I am happy you found Daniela. You must bring her over, she is family now, and Maman is still here, the holidays are close. Maybe a nice family dinner?" She played with her almost empty plate of food awhile I mulled things over.

CHAPTER 28: EPILOGUE

So, where does all this leave me. A point had come where I had to explain myself. I had to make my family understand what had been my motivation and what continues to be my motivation.

Lamashtu Anzillu.

Am I obsessed by her? Quite probably, but I would like to think it is with good reason. How can I communicate this, when there are so many questions in my mind? I did not have a childhood. My grandfather saw to it that such a simple thing would be beyond me. Why me? Why should I have to be the one who loses out on a childhood? But then, so did Alix. So did Adhémar. None of us were allowed that privilege, so perhaps I am not being indulgent when I want my own twins to have at least something of what I missed. Alix is no different when it comes to her daughter, Kati Eliana.

But Lamashtu Anzillu. A Sumerian demoness who has come to realise that the modern world holds much attraction to her. Wars, plagues, the greed of both individuals and nations. The human race is almost like an 'all you can eat' buffet for her.

And if my explanations seem sketchy in places, that is intentional. I had to find out what was happening around me, even if it felt as if I must fight with one hand tied behind my back. But, at least I have to try to stop her rampage. Just as within my birth pack, there are some who cannot protect themselves, so someone must step forward. Don't consider me a hero, because I am no hero. I am one Alpha wolf, who is fortunate to have had those who wish to side with me. However, the dichotomy remains. I must find out things the hard way. We all do.

And now, if you wish, turn the page for a sample of the next book, perhaps, in the series: Omega. Or maybe, it will be Part 2 of Fane's story: Yr Ddraig Goch.

<u>OMEGA</u>

Chapter 1:WAITING TO DIE

Talia was not, by nature, someone who admitted defeat, yet as she staggered to her feet after another round of violent convulsions, she found herself almost wishing that the end would come swiftly, finally easing her pain. She had done something wrong, misread something, pronounced something wrong. Exhaustion was leading to useless cyclic thinking, she shook her head and began to count backwards, she could now only hope that her poor judgement did not end up costing further lives.

Slight, hesitant, shuffling steps to the ancient basin had her splashing her face and washing the acidic taste from her mouth. As her eyes met the woman in the mirror, she felt her chest tighten, barely recognising the pitiful creature.

She needed far more than a spa day or a blowout she thought with a depreciating half smirk. Weight that she had not really needed to lose had melted off her frame in the passing days, muscle mass disappearing despite all her best efforts. Her honey gold skin had become sallow, the sickly yellow the seemed to offset the greyed bruising to a horrific advantage. She shuddered, though only partially from revulsion. Another chill had taken hold as a fever raged within her. If ever there was a case for reading the fine print, this would have been the one.

The drone of the television was temporarily drowned out by the running water as the young woman brushed her teeth. Despite the gruelling training she and her sisters were required to survive, she had not been prepared for this agony. Burning, throbbing, tearing waves, only to be made more acute after brief moments of respite. This was one of those moments, her stomach had eased, and she was able to catch her breath, perhaps that was the cruellest thing. To feel free, only to be shackled by pain, waves upon waves and never knowing when or if, there would be another reprieve.

There was no point in attempting to hide her illness, money had bought them an unused ward in a Brazilian hospital. She had produced documentation stating she was a personal physician and that her incredibly reclusive employer valued his privacy over all else. She had hoped that would have been enough to ensure their protection. However, one nurse had dared to sneak a peek, as she had insisted on delivering supplies to the ward, instead of leaving them at the agreed upon point just outside the doors. One look at doctor, and the patient had sent the human all but screaming and Talia could not have the unnecessary attention, compounding those sins she was most likely currently being punished for, the human female would just be another burden

She wasted little energy checking on her patient and beginning a new infusion set. For the most part he appeared to have entered some sort of stasis, he felt very little of what was happening, she reasoned as he no longer seemed to react to pain, his pale and greyed features almost appeared to be in slumber. Now it appeared she was singlehandedly bearing the physical effects, and when her physical form finally broke, they would both be off on their next and final journey. No one would mourn them, and eventually, the worst would happen, they would be expunged from memory, and truly become nothing.

She pushed back her waves of melancholia, choosing to focus on what she could continue to do in the present. So long as the magic held, and their money didn't run out they had access to a hospital dispensary, their pain signals could be dulled by powerful medications, tissue could be fed, and further deterioration could hopefully be slowed until she found a solution. By nourishing and strengthening the physical she was taking the smallest measure of hope that they could slow down the physical strains of what should inevitably end in their deaths.

When the machine had begun to click softly, she sighed softly and moved to cover him up, her palms brushing over his chest, hovering over his heart. Her throat tightened, the lump that settled in her throat becoming harder to swallow.

With a grimace, she took a deep breath and began preparing her own treatment. Food had lost its appeal when it avenged itself so violently and so she had begun to up her own infusion regimen. After settling onto her own Stryker bed she closed her eyes and began to attempt to supplement the pain medication through breathing and meditation. She could hear no longer the incessant chatter of the television, she was focused on each and every soft click, until blissfully, she drifted off to sleep.

-x-

Waking suddenly Talia bolted upright, heart pounding, orienting herself as quickly as her narcotic-saturated mind would allow.

Her eyes locked on a silent figure standing mere feet from her bed, she swallowed back an angry bark as she realized that the female watching her so intently had probably been there long enough to have killed both her and Kurt, multiple times over. So, antagonizing a being she could not identify, other than one of exceptional power, did not seem to be in either of their best interests. She was exhausted and weak and in no shape to defend either of them if the situation were to turn. She rose, and quickly turned off the machine, disconnecting the infusion set. She hated showing weakness but was too weary to have to find another good vein and begin again.

Her eyes were wary, but she lifted her chin, a silent challenge. She had not fought this hard to lose the battle now. She could feel the power radiating from this silent female, leaving Talia both frightened and intrigued.

"Are you here to help us?" Her voice held the tiniest thread of hope. Without a benefactor she knew her moments were measured.

She knew she had nothing with which to negotiate, but appearances were everything in her world and if she appeared to have more strength than she did, perhaps it would work in her favour. The fact that she was pretty much willing to agree to anything that did not result in their deaths at this point was irrelevant. She had nothing left but a vision of the future that in her pain wrecked nightmares she had begun to second guess.

Talia had always loved puzzles, games, and mysteries and while Kurt was darkly, and dangerously, handsome there were many males that fit that description in their world, and any number of them would have been far easier to work with, and work under. How could she explain to other people what she was thinking and feeling when it came to her Alpha when she really didn't understand it herself? Common sense told her to disconnect, that their partnership, if one could call it that had been cursed from its beginnings.

He had never been particularly kind to her, cool, curt, and often verbally scathing, and she had never quite mustered the courage to ask why he seemed to hate her so. Initially he had been at least thoughtful, but their Queen's interference had turned most of their interactions into nightmares. The

149

remainder of the time she could not read him. A tightened jaw might be the only indication that he gave that he even noticed she existed outside of their forced partnership, in deference to their Queen's wishes. Even then it seemed as if he were toying with her, never going so far as to disgrace her before Lamashtu herself, but he kept her guessing and off balance. No one would ever mistake them for being a cohesive team. He gave orders, she obeyed them. Their Queen gave orders, they both obeyed.

When she had begun to doubt herself and her own resolve then she placed faith in the sisters who had shared with her some of their visions, their reinforcement, the belief that their shared gifts would empower her to finish what she had started, that it was all for a purpose. She was having trouble keeping that in mind as she was now isolated from her sisters and spent more hours in agony than lucid.

If he chose, she still fervently hoped that she could convince him to forgive her for all of this, and to perhaps seize the opportunity to be the Alpha of her visions.

"I'm going to reason that you are not here to kill me. You most likely had plenty of time for that, but unless I miss my guess you could have, many times over. So, why didn't you?" Puzzled she watched the female, almost as intently as she was looking at her. A shiver slithered over her spine and unconsciously, she wrapped her arms across her chest, awaiting the female's reply.

Chapter 2: DREAMING

Kurt wasn't sure what he expected when the Anghelescu Justice's blade had pieced him. An end, surely. Checks and balances. That's what it was supposed to mean. And, when it came down to it, as strong as she was, Lamashtu was hardly a vision of sweetness and light. As her proverbial right arm, leading her Hellhound Pack, he had soiled his hands more than once.

Humans told themselves that eternal punishment awaited those of his nature. Yeah, this lack of sensation could be deemed a punishment, but Kurt had expected more. He didn't feel trapped, more that he was in stasis, waiting.

Waiting for what?

The Justice was supposed to be instant. Bam! That was it. You are judged. End of story. Here's your punishment to suffer for eternity. What would happen to his Pack under Anghelescu, he wondered? It was clear that the male had a relationship with his female. Her essence had the barrier that said she was Mated. What would it mean for Talia? Would she return to Lamashtu as one of her Omegas and would she be 'reassigned'? Did Anghelescu even appreciate what she was?

Kurt felt a sensation. He might have called it laughter. Omega. It implied so much and yet the actuality was more than a bit different from the common perception. Did Fane Anghelescu realise that with his own Omega? So many questions. Was that the justice? That he must spend eternity with all these questions buzzing though his mind, whilst his body remained immobile?

The mind was a curious thing after all.

Was that what would happen then? He must consider what might have occurred, before he was punished, so he knew which actions had damned him, and he must agonise over how circumstances could have been different. Yeah, that would be hell, to be unable to act, to watch all his decisions play out, without argument, without being able to explain the greatest question of all: why?

He had served his Queens to the best of his ability. Surely that counted for something. He had protected his Pack as well as he might. That must matter?

Instead, he just had ... nothing. No sight. No sound. All senses gone. Nothing. Watch the deaths, over and over. A spark lit within him. Would he have the opportunity to argue his case? Did whatever cosmic system ran things even care? Kurt found himself wanting it to be so.

CYSGODION

YR DDRAIG GOCH: an extract

Fane paused for a moment, looking for all the world that he was savouring the baguette in his hand. Instead he was extending his senses as an Alpha Hellhound. Something was watching him, and it was not something that was... well inclined towards him either. Fact that, if it thought Fane was going to bring it back to the bar, and his pack, it had another thing coming. One thing was clear: it had a distinct stink of a creature to whom he owed no allegiance.

"Jestan. Been a while since I smelled your particular stink. What brings you topside?" Fane turned slowly, knowing that his opponent could be in either of his two forms: human or dog. The latter made it easier to travel topside, since more often than not, the only thing a stray dog at worry about was the dog warden.

"She misses you Fane." Justin was in human form in this instance, his skin colour the pale coffee with cream colour of upper-class native of India, adopting a similar sort of look to the 'biker chic' of my own pack.

Fane thought back to the time that Jestan had been one of his trainers, teaching them to fight, but taking great pleasure in beating Fane down to the ground and making him bleed. Still, he had done Fane a favour, because they came a point when the bouts were between equals, rather than the master taking down the student. "You know as well as I that she can fuck off." Fane wanted to snarl his response, but that would have told Jestan that his comment had penetrated Fane's armour and given him an advantage.

"She will have you back." Jestan's tone was equally pleasant. "Scrap that. You are going back to her in chains, and she will make sure you regret every second of the last six months of your rebellion against her."

Fane laughed. "She might want to have me back in chains, but that just is not going to happen." Fane sneered at him, even as he drew his blade from some hidden scabbard on his back. "Particularly not if she sends a loser like you to attempt to take me."

Damn, but Fane was not going to manage to enjoy his baguette after all, as he manifested a weapon of his own, all four foot of glowing blade, the red hell flames dancing up and down in their own pattern, a physical manifestation of the power Fane had gathered from the late human guest. "Bring it on." Fane invited his opponent, pleasantly.

-x-

When Fane walked back to his bar, he had a new burn mark down the side of his face, and his formally pristine designer leather jacket looked like it had been to hell and back. The burn on his leg was causing him to limp slightly, but it would heal. Jestan was not exactly a picture of prettiness either, but clearly Fane needed to send a message back to the Queen, and in terms she would understand quite clearly.

Throughout the bout, Jestan had tried to force Fane's anger, tried to taunt him with promises of what he would watch the Queen do to him, when Fane was returned to her in chains. He had reminded Fane of how many of the scars on his back he had both witnessed the Queen putting them there herself and how many of them Jestan himself had put there, with not all of them being from fight practice. The Queen had intended that Fane might be ready to fight any attack, and that meant that he had endured every form of attack, with weapons and without. And, if she wanted to reward one of her pets, then what better reward was there and watch them take their pleasure of her Alpha Designate, whom she knew would take what was given, all in the name of protecting his sister and keeping his own oaths. Never mind that, even at that stage, Lamashtu had already broken her side of the deal. To their former Queen, that was a minor detail in the face of her pleasure. That his opponent thought that the reminders might raise Fane's anger was quite true. But what he had not considered was that when Fane had held his sister as she died, the fire of anger had turned ice, and ice that would not prevent him from thinking clearly. Thus, anger never clouded his judgement and his Pack was better protected for it.

No, rather than raise Fane's anger, all that had done was remind him of everything he had endured to protect his sister and all for nothing. Nothing was sweeter than demonstrating just what he thought of all that he had endured, particularly when it had been for nothing. So, as he walked into the Chain & Sprocket bar, it looked as if Fane had been in a fight. The sentinel behind the bar had merely passed Fane a half tumbler full of Scotch whiskey, undiluted. Continuing to his usual booth, Fane waited for Stefania to return.

For her part there was something about the evening air that always managed to calm Stefania. The cool night air kissing her arms, the wind blowing softly in her hair and the whisper of a breeze across the neck. It was one of the best feelings in the world. She made her way back to the bar slowly. Part of her wanted to go and see Lucien herself but Fane would be expecting her back and she didn't like to keep him waiting. When she finally walked through the door her eyes scanned automatically for her Alpha. She felt a slight disappointment that he had yet to return.

Nodding her head in thanks to the barman for sliding a beer across to her, Stefania took a quick drink. No, she couldn't stay there. She could smell the humans on her. Fane would be angry, or at least assume something had happened. The last thing Stefania needed was to fight with him tonight. Leaving a beer on the side, Stefania moved to the back into the bar and into Fane's office. It was there that she felt it. Something was wrong. Really wrong. Ice cold anger, and emotion, and instinct, the need. It took her by surprise and it almost had heard doubled over with the intensity of it, but within seconds it had gone, as if it never happened. Stefania hadn't realised how hard she had been gripping onto the desk until she realised her fingerprints were imprinted into the delicate wood.

She tried to distract herself with thoughts unrelated to what had just happened. It had nothing to do with the Queen, or the poison or anything else to do with past events. That was behind her now. The trauma she had suffered was all in the past. Stefania shuddered, not only on the outside of her body but inside as well. The smell of blood hit her like a wave. She knew that smell. It… It was Fane. She ran out of the room down the corridor, into the bar. He was there, trying to sit down in the booth they shared. Stefania stormed over, the rage she felt was beyond normal for a Beta's loyalty to her Alpha.

"What the FUCK happened?" She demanded.

Stefania was shaking, physically. Who would dare put their hands on Fane? Who would be even be stupid enough to think of such a thing? She grabbed his face and tilted it to the side to examine the mark decorating it. "A burn?" She moved in, her face falling to his shoulder, so that the scent hit her before she needed to be that close. Stefania knew that smell. Immediately a growl rose in her throat. "I'll kill him."

Before Fane could even stop her, Stefania was walking towards the door. If Fane had already dealt with him, it would mean she had a very good chance of doing additional damage with very little risk to herself.

Under the circumstances given that it had taken Fane long enough to sit down, and standing would just take as long, he extended his hand and froze Stefania taking control of the major muscles. It was not something he did too often not least because it was a waste of energy to deal with the pissed-off Hellhound, and she was going to be pissed off. Working his way out from the booth, and leaving his whiskey on the table, Fane limped towards her.

Yet it was safe to say that his Beta was now beyond angry with him. Still better that than he risked going after Jestan, knowing that the attack had occurred on the orders of their former Queen. Lamashtu would be ecstatic to have Fane's Beta in her hands, and by Herne's balls, Fane was not going to lose another Beta to that psychopathic bitch. "No Stefania, you are not going after him. I have already sent him back to our former Queen, with a clear message of how I viewed her attempted attack." Releasing her, Fane pulled Stefania close. "I will not lose another Beta to that bitch and I will not lose you in particular."

Thoughts swirled around Stefania's mind as she considered what she was going to do to the demon who dared lay hands on her Alpha. On her Fane. She was almost at the door and the rage inside her was beyond boiling point when her entire body froze. What the hell? She couldn't move. It dawned on her like a blow to the face. He wouldn't. He wouldn't dare use this cheap trick on her again, she thought. But to Stefania's horror Fane appeared in front of her. He must have been able to tell by the loathing in her eyes how angry she was. He knew how much Stefania hated being controlled like this. If he thought taking her into his arms would have distracted her from the anger at what he had done, he was wrong. The moment he lifted his compulsion, Stefania slapped him across the face, hard and with the full weight of her anger behind it. "Don't ever do that to me again. I am not just another member of your pack. I am your Beta and I deserve better than that!"

Stefania stormed away from him before she did any more damage to him personally, letting out a scream of rage. Changing her mind, she stormed back over to him, her face was inches away from his. "You should have told me. I could have helped. You are no use to us we can." Placing her hands on her hips, Stefania struggled to regain her breathing under control. "You can heal yourself tonight."

Stefania looked Fane up and down with pure anger woven through her entire body. She wanted to scream to hurt him, to push him out of the way and tell him to go fuck off while she went after Jestan anyway. She had a feeling Fane wasn't going to get out of the way until she had moved from the door, so Stefania moved, sending the bar contents spilling onto the floor as she did. Mature? Yes, she knew, but she needed to release her anger somehow. She went back into the office and slammed the door behind her.

Fane raised his hand to the side of his face where Stefania had slapped him. He had a wry grin on his face. Damn, but his little Hunter was on fire tonight, and potential for injury notwithstanding, he liked it. Just as well she had hit him on the side that didn't have the burn. Still, the problem he had was that such displays of temper with the very thing that meant that, eventually, he had to administer an Alpha's discipline on his sister and then Beta. It would be best to nip that in the bud sooner rather than later

And 'heal himself tonight'? Fane laughed mirthlessly. No way.

Without a word, Fane followed Stefania into his office, making sure that the mantle of power that marked him as Alpha was more than visible to the pack. They needed to see this as an Alpha having words with his Beta, rather than an Alpha going after a bit of tail.

"Stefania, I did not do that to humiliate you. That demon is not worth your effort, and in any case, I have already sent him back. Our former Queen would enjoy nothing more than to have her talons on you." Fane took a breath. "She killed my sister because Roxana tried to protect me. Think for a moment, on what she would have done to you? She may not control us anymore, but if you go downstairs you are in her domain, and she will make sure you know it."

Stefania had heard him coming behind her, but she didn't turn around to look at him. She didn't want to see him right now. She didn't know if it was the wild care he played about the

Queen or if he was ignoring the simple fact, that he was demanding she did nothing about him being hurt, when she knew only too well if the roles had been reversed no matter what she had said or done, he would have gone to defend her. Stefania sulked even lower into her mood. She didn't want to be a source of worry for Fane but by him undermining her authority and taking away from her like that, especially in front of the whole bar, it was something she was struggling to overcome.

"You know the situation, how some still challenge my position as Beta and your actions tonight would have done nothing more than encourage their behaviour."

Stefania turned, despite promising herself that she wouldn't. He looked like hell. He really did. His one cheek was red thanks to her angry outburst, the other was still weeping with blood and he wasn't standing in his usual dominant stance. Damn. She knew she shouldn't have turned around.

"Next time … Next time, screw your compulsion. I will go and kill the bastard myself. We clear?"

Aware that it could have been taken as a direct challenge, Stefania's eyes softened, no longer holding the anger that they once did. She never could hold her anger long around Fane. Whether he used his abilities to calm her or simply just the way he was looking at her, it would evaporate as quickly as it came on. "You can't expect me to be okay with you being hurt, because I'm not and I never will be." Stefania realised this was getting deep, when her fingers traced around the burn, wanting to erase it. Especially so close after having a fight. She changed her attack. "Especially when I'm the one who has to heal you. Which I won't be… Not tonight. I might freeze up." She gave Fane a sarcastic smile. If he thought he could get away with freezing her without an apology, he could whistle for his feed.

Stefania realised it was impossible to stay angry with Fane when he was so talented with his words. He always knew what to say, the right things at exactly the right time. She couldn't stay angry with him forever. Stefania accepted why he did what he did and even understood the reasoning behind it. Maybe it was just because of that reason that she found herself walking towards him accepting the hug he offered. His arms felt so safe, sometimes Stefania wondered why she was ever able to leave them? Her own arms snaked around his neck and with it he received the forgiveness he was looking for. Gently raising her head to peer up at him, her eyes were able to properly examine the nasty burn mark, carved into the side of his face. "I hope to all that is holy you sent him home looking worse than you did."

"Stefania, little Hunter, I apologise for what I did. It was impulsive, the very thing I try to avoid doing." Fane closed the distance slightly between them. As Stefania turned to face him, Fane opened his arms to her. Deliberately he did not take her in his arms but wanted to give her the choice to come closer to him. "I know that by preventing you from taking revenge for the attack, I prevented you from fulfilling the role of Beta to which I appointed you. And yes, I know that in doing so I undermined your authority. Again, for that I apologise." Fane had a half smile on his face. "But I will not apologise for wanting to keep you safe. Knowing what that damn Lupei Queen did to you before, the thought that our own former Queen might do the same, for no other reason than to cause us both pain, fills me with dread. My decision was the lesser of two evils, but it is still an evil for all that." The smile faded from his lips. "We need to warn the pack of what has happened. The Queen has clearly decided that in leaving us the six months, we will have grown complacent and thought ourselves safe now that we are topside. She hoped that she would catch as unprepared. The others need to be aware of that."

Fane laughed. "By Herne's balls, we might even end up working with the damned Cŵn Annwn."

It was the remark about the Queen that made Stefania stiffen in his embrace. For some reason she had been under the impression that the demon had attacked Fane in an unprovoked surprise attempt to claim some questionable credit with the Queen. It hadn't crossed her mind that the Queen could have... No... She sent Jestan with the notion of deliberately harming Fane. This was meant as a warning.

Stefania nodded, wanting to agree with him but deep down she didn't like this at all. Something big was coming and she just hoped they were going to be prepared for it.

"Talking of the Cŵn Annwn, weren't we supposed to be visiting this Lucien?" Desperately trying to change the conversation, Stefania removes her arms around him and moved to the desk sitting on the edge of it. "I can go if you like, shake up a bit. I doubt he will be in possession of the drug plus by the time you limp over there, he may have died or grown senile with old age." Stefania gave Fane a sarcastic smile. "Unless you were planning on coming with me? Because if that's the case and you don't want to keep your war wounds, I suggest you get over here and kiss me within the next 10 seconds."

Fane gave Stefania another one of his half smile is at her words, that really, he needed to deal with the visible injuries left by his encounter with Jestan and as an incubus, that method of healing himself was so very pleasurable. "By all means Stefania. I can't have my decrepit body slowing down your interrogations of this Lucien." Lowering his lips to hers, Fane nibbled his way around her mouth, before claiming Stefania's lips, and as the hunger for his little Hunter seized him, he felt the surge of strength that resulted from the passion in 'just a kiss'.

Raising his head, Fane could feel the small surge of energy start to work, as the flesh seared by the burn started to knit together, capillaries sealing, the cells of the dermis finding within themselves to regenerate. He knew that in a matter of seconds the burn on his face would be a faint scar, just another souvenir of a battle won. "My thanks, Stefania." He murmured, still holding her. "Now, if we are to continue this...healing, then perhaps we had best go see what this pawn shop owner has to tell us?"

Stefania nodded, returning his smile. "Let's go kick some ass."

DIARIES OF THE CŴN ANNWN

A Final Word for Jo

Every cloud has a silver lining. This book, along with several others hopefully, was published during the 2020 Covid-19 lock-down, when I was on furlough from my day job managing a branch of The Works.

What started as a means to deal with the loneliness of working away from home as a medical representative became something much more. But it would not have grown had it not been for people buying my books, whether from the e-book outlets or via Kindle Unlimited.

Either way, thank you.

As you know, reviews are the lifeblood of part-time authors like me. They enable our books to be seen, they move us up the ranking. Equally, those who are kind enough to point out mistakes to me personally, rather than reporting it to the great 'Zon, have done me a great service. With your help, the world of the Cŵn Annwn will continue to grow.

If you do want to contact me, this is how:

Facebook: www.facebook.com/JoPilsworthAuthor
Twitter: @jopilsworth
LinkedIn: www.linkedin.com/JoPilsworth

DIARIES OF THE CŴN ANNWN

Printed in Poland
by Amazon Fulfillment
Poland Sp. z o.o., Wrocław